Making Ends Meat

by Michael Fairclough

To Gaylord

Making Ends Meat
First published in 2023
by Converge, an imprint of the Writing Tree

All rights reserved. No part of this publication may be reproduced, stored in a database or retrieval system, or transmitted, in any form or by any means, without the prior permission in writing of the publisher, nor be otherwise circulated in any form or binding or cover other than that in which it is published and without a similar condition including this condition being imposed on the subsequent purchaser.

© 2023 Michael Fairclough
Cover art also © 2023 Michael Fairclough

The moral rights of the author has been asserted.
All characters and events in this publication, other than those clearly in the public domain, are fictitious, and any resemblance to any real person, living or dead, is purely coincidental and not intended by the author.

For information contact:
Writing Tree Press,
Unit 10773, PO Box 4336
Manchester, M61 0BW
www.writingtree.co.uk

Contents

TROUBLE IN PARADISE	7
PULLED OVER	9
WINDOW	11
FOOTBALL	14
COME DINE ON ME	16
CLOTHES SHOPPING	20
GIFT	23
ADVERTS	25
EMERGENCY DISPATCHER	26
DUSTY ROAD	28
FLIGHT SCHOOL	30
NEW HOUSE	33
ONE PLEASE	34
DANCER	36
SECRET	37
SUICIDE?	38
TURTOISE	41
SURGERY	42
SOCIAL LIVES	44
FISHFAIR?	47
VASECTOMY	49
I KNOW A GUY	51
BIG SHOES	53
NEW BAR	54

TRAP	55
TRESPASSING	56
SCARECLOWN	58
WHAT IS LOVE?	59
COPE	67
HOSPITAL	69
FIRED	71
MESSAGE	73
TAKEAWAY	75
JOBS	77
FAMILY FRIEND	79
THE OFFICE	82
LOST PROPERTY	85
DISGRACED	88
MAKING A STAND	90
TIS THE SEASON	91
THERAPY	93
NEW JOB	95
SECURITY GUARD	97
HOME IMPROVEMENT	99
LATE FOR WORK	100
SONAR DATING	101
CHILDHOOD'S END	105
POST	122
THERAPY SESSION TWO	124
SANTAS - PLURAL	127

LAST WORDS	135
WHEN I EAT MYSELF	138
FAKE	142
WITNESS	143
WHAT DO YOU THINK YOU ARE?	145
GLUE	148
MULEAN	167
THE GRAND NUSIANCE	172
COURT	189
FISHING TRIP	190
SEX, DRUGS AND MASHED POTATO	192
WALLET	197
DINNER	199
HORSEMEAT	201
THE KING OF THE HUMBLED	218
ROOM	232
THE SMALL GUYS	233
LATE	235
BAD NEWS	236
HUNGRY FOR CHRISTMAS	237
WHAT IS LOVE? – PART DEUX	241
EPILOGUE BY TIM	253
G-OATS	254
HOW WE MET	255
MORE SURGERY	256
ASHES	257

GLOBAL WARMING	258
REAL CRIME	259
BUTTOWL VILLAGE GROSSERYS	262
FUNERAL	266
PERSONALS	268
FARM	270
COATS	274
BABE IN THE WOODS	277
SPACE	279
ACKNOWLEDGEMENTS	285
ABOUT MICHAEL FAIRCLOUGH	287

TROUBLE IN PARADISE

I was at my wit's end and had tried everything, even that golf ball thing, but alas my hens would just not lay. Needing some air, I went for a walk out in my fields when I saw Roy in the field over.

"Now then, Pete, everything okay? You seem troubled."

Walking over to him, I noticed there was a clown hiding in one of the dividing bushes watching us. Roy was a mean one like that.

"Now then, Roy, you're a smart cookie. You know owt 'bout getting hens to lay?"

"You try golf balls?"

"Yeah."

"Typical, that's the golf ball manufacturers for you - lies upon lies. A horrible practice. Say, you're lucky you caught me, though. I have the answer to your problems, Pete."

"Really? You're not screwing with me? What do I need to do?"

"Tell me - do you have any candles?"

"Candles? What am I meant to do with them, smoke the eggs out?"

"No, you twit. You need them to set the mood - a bit of romantic music, a few candles. Maybe even dress up nice, if you know what I mean?"

"Not really. Well, everything but the dress up nice. That sounds rather like you're insinuating something."

"Oh, yeah. I forgot. You ain't married, are you? Let me spell it out for you. mate - you need some

LINGERIE."

"Lingerie?"

"Yep. Drives them wild."

"And where do you suggest I get some lingerie from?"

As it turns out Roy had quite the selection.

PULLED OVER

It was a cold November night, and me and my wife had just set off from a funeral when the flashing lights came on behind me. Checking the mirror, I saw it was a patrol car of the local County sheriff. Being a new citizen in the country, I decided to pull over and get my licence and registration ready. Best not cause a fuss, I thought to myself, as the officer strolled up.

"Hello, sir. Do you know why I pulled you over tonight?" he said, in that authoritative tone that marks every one of them.

Making a stab in the dark, I guessed, "Is it the dead body?"

"Bingo," he replied in a most chipper manner, then went on to lecture me on my incompetence.

"Now, sir, don't get me wrong - everybody has to transport a body at some point in their life, but improper safety when transporting said body is negligence while operating a vehicle. Do you know how many accidents a year are caused by people failing to strap things down properly?"

I chose to be honest with the man.

"No, I'm sorry, officer, I don't. To be candid I have not been myself as of late."

"I understand," he said, dropping his professional manner and showing emotion for the first time. "Tell you what, sir - I will let you off with a caution this time but think next time, eh? Now, just you wait there a second. I think I may have something we can secure her with. Don't want to lose her again, eh?"

Relieved at his understanding, I took him up on his offer.

"Thank you so much, officer."

"That's okay, sir. Everyone needs a hand every now and again. If it's not too painful, may I ask what happened to her?"

Reluctantly, I told him. "She was shot in the head and chest repeatedly."

The look on his face turned to shock, then puzzlement, and then the look of someone you know has something to say.

"Wow, she's looking good for it."

"Yeah. I hired the best taxidermist I could find, and he did a fantastic job with her. You know, it's ironic, really. We moved to England to get away from the gun violence and then, one day as she was taking the cubs to school, a SWAT team pulled up, got out and shot her, Little Winnie and Paddington 2 dead."

"Well, you have my condolences, sir. I'm about all done, my side. I'll let you get on home, yeah? You stay safe." Thoroughly assisted, he walked back to his car and drove off into the night. Truthfully, though, despite the sadness I felt discussing my wife and children's deaths, I wish he'd stayed a while longer as I found it cathartic, and he seemed to be a man of great understanding.

The fact is, I can't bear to be alone these days.

WINDOW

I had just taken my morning shower and walked into my bedroom to get dressed when it started: an unnatural sound of horrific connotations emanating from my window. Unsure how to proceed, I decided to seek the guidance of my wife. Unfortunately, she was out of the country on business. Not knowing what else could be done, I risked her ire and called her. The phone began to ring, the tone continuing in regular increments to remind me of its presence. Growing impatient, I began to chant to myself a prayer of sorts.

"Pick up, pick up, pick up, pick up." On my fourth 'pick up' my wife replied.

"Hello?"

"SHANNON! Shannon, thank Dog," I whispered – well, intended to.

"David? Is that you? Do you realize what time it is here?"

"But I'm scared Shannon."

"What's wrong now, David?"

"There's something outside our window making an unspeakable sound. It's like letch letch ehehehe letch letch ehehehe but not that, as it's unspeakable. I'd just got out of the shower and came into our room to get dressed when it started."

"Okay, calm down. Now, David, what exactly do you want me to do?"

"Oh, come to think of it there is nothing you can do. I'm all alone. I'm all alone, Shannon!" I almost lost it, and my heart rate began to rise, only settling when Shannon distracted me with a question.

"Wait - what day is it there?"

Unsure of her motive for asking, I replied with hesitation.

"Wednesday?"

"It's the new window cleaner, David."

"Are you sure? It doesn't sound like a window cleaner."

"Well, if it's Wednesday morning, I'm 99.9% certain it's him."

Somewhat reassured by this, I began to compose myself but realized I had yet to face my fear. At this point, Shannon seemed to realize this and proceeded to tell me to face it.

"Just open the bloody curtains, David, and see for yourself. It's daylight there after all."

"Okay, Shannon - I'm going to do it now."

"Wonderful."

I began to count to Shannon, mouthpiece still to my head.

"Three...two...one ... ARGH!!"

"DAVID! DAVID WHAT'S WRONG? SPEAK TO ME!" Shannon shouted down the phone, unreasonably loud.

"There is a giraffe at the window." My mind raced for anything else to say but Shannon spoke again.

"See, I told you it was the window cleaner."

I was aghast at how flippant she was.

"You didn't say he was a giraffe, Shannon," I retorted.

"You do realize I can hear you through the glass, don't you, sir?" the giraffe interjected, shocking me once more with this fresh revelation.

"SHANNON! THE GIRAFFE CAN HEAR ME!"
Once again he interjected, talking over Shannon.
"I can see you, as well, sir."
And that's when I remembered I was still naked.

FOOTBALL

We go now to the after-match press conference with Cow-Liverpool's new manager, Benjamin Pinder.

"Ben, Ben!"

"Yes, you - the hedgehog."

"Hi, Armando - the Daily Rooster. So, Ben, how do you think the team did with the first match of the season?"

"Okay. I mean, we did win after all, and the whole herd really pulled together in the second half."

"And what do you think was the reason for your comeback exactly?"

"Probably that we took the bells off. They can be quite distracting."

"Ben! Ben!"

"Yes. You - the zebra in a trilby."

"Thanks. Ned, the Daily Weekly. How do you feel the other team did, given the obvious disadvantage they had coming in?"

"Well, that's the thing about Bat-Man United. They are generally a lot smaller, but that's not necessarily a bad thing, as they can dodge and weave. Then again, regrettably they do suffer a lot of injuries having to head the ball most of the time."

"Ben! Ben! What do you think of the allegations of you milking your cows before the game?"

"Well, even if it's true, it's a natural process unlike what I hear about them blood suckers."

"What – they suck blood?"

"Yes! Exactly!"

"Ben, Ben! Do you think we will see you win any

more games this year?"

"Well, I'm ever the orthodontist and, at the end of the day, if the team does poorly, I can just send them to the slaughterhouse."

"Don't you mean optimist?"

"No more questions."

We go now over to Bat-Manchester United with their Manager, David Brady.

"Give it to me Brady, Aha Aha, give it to me, Brady. What do you think is the source of your team's losing streak?"

"Probably all the concussions. They tend to get trod on a lot."

COME DINE ON ME

Today on *Come Dine on Me*, will Nora be able to keep her family out of the kitchen while trying to host at the same time? And will Harold have improved his manners since the fiasco at Suzanna's? This and more on *Come Dine on Me*.

"So, Nora, how's the cooking going? Do you think it will be done in time for the guests arriving?"

"Well, maybe if you left me alone and took the bloody camera crew out of the kitchen."

Opting to film from the garden, we took the chance to interview Nora's neighbour.

"So, have you ever had the chance to try Nora's cooking?"

"No."

"Anything else you would like to say? This is for a television show!"

"Hi Mum, no wait she's dead. Hi Da.. no, I killed him to. Can you come back to me later?"

Back at the kitchen window, we caught up with Nora.

"So, Nora, can you talk us through what you are doing now?"

"Well, in order to get the prize, I figured I would go for something popular and ever versatile."

"And that is?"

"Chicken, but to be specific - a katsu curry, with a special twist."

"Interesting. So, tell us, what's the twist?"

"Sod off, you can wait for it like everyone else.

Besides I need to get some eggs in private."

"I see."

Just then the doorbell rang, so we made our way round to the front to greet the first guest and get let back in.

"Harold, welcome!"

"Ah! The hell were you doing, watching me from the bushes? I weren't pissing, promise."

"We just came from around the back of the house."

"Right. Why's that?"

"We got kicked out of the kitchen again."

"Ha. I did try knocking, by the way."

"Oh, I think she went to the bog. She said she needed some eggs and wanted some privacy."

"Well, isn't that a lovely image?"

After doing her business, Nora let us inside again and we talked to Harold for a bit in the dining room as he reflected on his night serving.

"So, now your dinner is out of the way, how do you feel about killing your daughter?"

"I'm not going to lie. It hit me quite hard, you know? After spending all that time raising her to have Suzanna asking for her steak well done. Like what the fuck is that, you know? Oh, sorry. Can I swear?"

"We can beep it out in post."

"Oh, good. Anyhow like who the fuck does she think she is? She is eating someone's daughter for goodness sake. The least she could ask for was bloody."

Harold's rant was out the way just in time, as Suzanna arrived next.

"Hi, guys. Oh, my Dog, Harold - you're here already. Awesome. I hope you're not seeing red any more, hahahahaha."

Intervening, we took Suzanna into the hallway to ask how she feels about her meal being next.

"Well, personally, I think I have it in the bag - the feeding bag, hahahahaha. In all seriousness, though, I used to work in a Wetherspoons so I think they're fucked. Hahahahaha"

"And have you picked which of your children you will be using for your main?"

"Duh, of course I have. Little Mike. He's been doing shit at his GCSEs so he's probably screwed, anyhow."

At that moment we had to stop and move out of the way as Nora brought through her strangled daughter's plucked corpse to start her main. Back in the dining room you could cut the tension with a knife. Thankfully, that's when the current lead arrived, and the atmosphere changed for the better.

"Sammy! Nice to see you."

"Hello, everyone. Harold, your horns look fantastic. Did you polish them especially?"

"I had them waxed."

"Well, they look great! And Suzanna, you look like you have been on holiday since yesterday."

"Yeah. I went for a tan. Good, ain't it?"

"Yes, very orange and good like the sun."

That out of the way, it was time for starters.

"Oh, hi, Nora. That looks nice. What is it?"

"Deviled egg, Sammy."

"Oh. Don't you have anything else? I'm allergic to egg."

"No, Suzanna, I don't. And if you are so allergic, why didn't you say something when they asked you about your preferences?"

"Uh, fine if you're going to be all mardy - but egg gives me gas, so you'll be sorry."

Starters over, we checked in with the kitchen from the garden.

"So, how's it going?"

"What happens to the rest of us?"

"Sorry what?"

"When this is over, what happens to the losers?"

"That would be telling. Don't you like a twist?"

CLOTHES SHOPPING

What's it like selling clothes? A job like any other, I suppose, but given our speciality we like to offer a personal touch with our services. Of course, we still have the awkward customers, the ones we can't satisfy, if you know what I mean. I recall one customer in particular. He seemed so oblivious to his antics that I ended up with two black eyes. If I remember correctly, he was shopping for something for his employee.

"Hello there, sir. You appear to be a bit lost. Is there anything I can help you with today?" I said, throwing the rest of the clothes I was stacking to the floor and kicking them under the bottom shelf.
"That would be much appreciated. I'm out of my field of expertise, so to speak," he replied turning around rather abruptly. That's when I noticed his shotgun over his shoulder as it swung around and hit me in the face knocking me into the discount lace panties rather abruptly. Offering me a hand to get up, I took it as I wiped the blood off on extra medium pair of the knickers.

"Okay, then what exactly are you looking for?" I said as I spat out a tooth and continued. "Something for the wife? Girlfriend, maybe?"

"They are more like an employee. To be honest, it's going to be something like a uniform for them,"

"Really? Well, there's a first for everything. Let's see what we can find, shall we? Where would you like to start? How do shoes sound?" I asked him, still holding his hand.

"I suppose it's as good as anything else. Do you have any heels?"

"Yes, we carry a wide selection. Do you know what size shoe she takes?"

"Large?"

"That's a no then? How about I show you a few options and you can see what you think works? You can always return them." I gestured to where we keep our shoes with my free hand.

"Yes, I guess. I will need two pairs, though." He finally noticed our intertwined fingers before promptly pulling his back and sniffing it.

Free at last, I strode across to our new selections and told him, "That shouldn't be a problem, how about these? They're new in and they come in larger sizes." He dashed over to join me, then abruptly stopped, but his gun's momentum kept going, swinging up and smacking down on my head.

"They're nice enough but they seem a bit heavy for her," he said, offering a hand to help me up yet again before sanitizing his hands with a gel. "She is a bit on the heavier side."

"Ah, okay then. Do you perchance know what she weighs?" I asked, only for him to say he would have to ring her up and ask, causing him to about face and, yet again, slap me with the barrel of his gun before walking out to make a call. Some time later he returned from outside the storefront with my answer.

"About two thousand pounds, give or take."

Unfortunately, we only carried our bulkier options for ten thousand pounds up and so, feeling the sale slipping, I changed the subject.

"Bras?"

"Well, that sounds more like it."

"Excellent. What cup size is she?"

"Four."

"Four what?"

"Four cups. Funny, really - I was looking at bras when you came up to me but they're all the wrong shape."

"...The wrong shape, sir?"

"Well, they all only have two cups. Seems a bit stupid to buy them separate when she has four. It's like you're running some sort of con. Us farmers aren't as wealthy as you think, you know." The conviction in his eyes was going, when inspiration hit me like his gun did, yet again, as he turned to leave.

"Wait! I have an idea!" I shouted before running into the back room and slapping together a new bra.

"Tada!" I was honestly quite pleased with it as I handed it to him for inspection.

"Oh, it's got four cups now. How did you do that? Oh, I see," he said, not impressed "Duct Tape, really?" He said handing the bra back by the cups before turning to leave. There was just one small snag however as the bra strap caught on his guns trigger and blew a chunk out of my leg.

"You shot me, you bloody shot me!"

"Oh dear, can't be in customer service talking like that. I think I will have to call your manager about you. Get you a shock collar or something."

GIFT

I first moved to Scarborough in 1978, after marrying the love of my life, Sally, the year before. We decided on Scarborough primarily to be near her family. I was happy enough to go along with it, as my job didn't require me to be in any sprawling metropolis, and I would be fine anywhere as long as I was with her.

These were the thoughts that ran through my mind one Friday as I debated getting off the train as it dawdled at the penultimate station. Eventually, I decided I would get off as it would be faster to swim, and I couldn't wait to see my wife as I had bought her a gift. On arriving home, I swam into the kitchen where I found my wife floating above the table.

"Craig, I wasn't expecting you back for a bit yet," she said.

"I figured I would surprise you and, speaking of surprises, close your eyes - I have something for you." As she closed her eyes, I dug through my rucksack 'til I found her gift and placed it on the table in front of her.

"Now open them," I whispered. Her mouth dropped slowly letting a small bubble escape into the room. She was ecstatic, I could tell, and after all, she had always been jealous of mine.

"Craig, you bought me fish fingers! Oh, my Dog! Help me put them on so I can wear my wedding ring."

"Okay, let me just find the instructions."

"Wait. Hold on."

"Yes, dear?"

"It says '8-pack, opposable thumbs sold separately'."

"Curse you, Birdseye!"

ADVERTS

New from Birdseye
Birdseye's bird eyes
Are you a pirate?
Are you a parrot?
Have your eyes been pecked out by a peckish, pirate, parrot?
Birdseye's bird's eyes, one size fits all

New from Birdseye
Birdseye's voluptuous thighs and lower legs
Been in an incident at sea?
Your woodworker wounded wildly in a wrath?
Hopping mad?
Birdseye's voluptuous thighs and lower legs
A cut above the rest

New from Birdseye
Incontinent off the continent?
Got a leak below the deck?
Birdseyes butt plu.. what do you mean, 'watershed'?

EMERGENCY DISPATCHER

A lot of people say to me it must be kind of boring when you are not dealing with emergencies, or just annoying having to deal with the time wasters and, yes, but then there are the calls that we are just not equipped for. I remember one that was particularly frustrating, as there was nothing we could do except give her some advice. I believe it went something like this:

"Hello. 999. What's your emergency?"

"There's a fish in my fish pond!"

"Okay. Can you elaborate please, madam?"

"I haven't had fish in my fish pond since my last ones got electrocuted."

"Okay, can I just ask, is the fish threatening you or being aggressive towards you in any way?"

"No, the few words we exchanged have been quite polite. He even invited me in, but I had my slippers on."

"Okay, so is it just the trespassing that's bothering you?"

"Well, yes. I did ask him if he would leave, but he said he had every intention of staying there as I was not using the space."

"Okay, could you describe him to me please?"

"Big Shark."

"Okay. So, I'm afraid what you have there is nothing we can help you with."

"So, what do you suggest I do?"

"Well, it would appear he is claiming exercising rights."

"Squatter's rights? It's my bloody fish pond!"

"Yeah, you should probably hire a lawyer. It's the best way to deal with land sharks."

At that, the woman hung up with understandable frustration and I went on with my shift. I do recall, however, seeing a headline in the local paper a few months later about a shark winning a court case but it might have been to do with that whole swimming pool controversy that's been going on. Personally, I think they should get out to use the toilets like everyone else. Now, as for the second question, I would say the most horrific call I had was one I had my first year on the job. It really caught me off guard.

"999. What's your emergency?"

"My wife's eating my babies."

"Oh, shit. That is an emergency. Who should we send? I'm thinking either police or ambulance, or both. You?"

"Animal control, the police and an ambulance."

"That's a bit rude, sir. She is your wife, after all."

"She's a hamster, you moron."

"Oh. In that case, you should ring Animal Control directly."

"But it's an emergency. An animal needs controlling and she's eating my babies, for goodness sake."

"Well, unless they are human babies, I'm not sure there is anything I can do for you."

"They are! I won them at the Fishfair."

DUSTY ROAD

"Excuse me, I don't suppose you are off to Bethlehem, are you?"

"Yes, I am, as a matter of fact."

"Oh, good show. I don't suppose you would like to split the fare?"

"Well, I was meant to meet two friends here, but they appear to have gone on without me. Then again, I have no idea what the time is. I've been drinking since dinner time. Shhhh."

"I did not need to know any of that."

"Oh, sorry. Yes, I will split the fare."

"Fantastic, and there's a taxi now. Yo, over here taxi!"

"Where to, lads?"

"Four to Bethlehem, please."

"Bethlehem. Anywhere in particular in Bethlehem, or are you just going to show up at some random inn?"

"Oh, just follow that star."

"Okay..."

A while later:

"Okay, chaps, that will be 800 shekels."

"800 shekels? That's outrageous."

"What can I say? You're the ones who wanted taking out to Bethlehem in the middle of the night on some wild goose chase about a star."

"Fine."

"And it's Christmas so that doubles it, as well."

"I said fine! okay, lads, what do we have? I have gold but it's a gift."

"Well I have frankincense, but it's a gift, too."

"Okay. What about you, Jaz?"

"I have a copy of the Metro I picked up earlier and some chewing gum."

"Wait, you got him a copy of the Metro? How cheap are you?"

"I just thought I could put my name on one of you guys' gifts, to be honest."

"You cheap sod."

"Look, never mind that now. We can call at the shops when we are done here."

"Hang on. What about the prat in the crown we shared the taxi with? I bet he's loaded."

"Yeah, good thinking. Hey, where did he go?"

"He bolted as soon as we got here."

"And you just let him?"

"I thought he was off to the toilet. His crown did fall off on that sand dune, though, so he might come back."

"Oh, nice. Serves him right, the snake. Yo, Donkey - you want this crown?"

"I guess. Put it on. I want to see what it's like first."

"Okay, I guess I can."

"No not you! Me, you idiot."

"Huh. Lighter than I expected, but it will do. You got off lucky this time, lads. See you around."

"Hey, Mel."

"What, Jaz?"

"Is it me, or did that crown say Burger King on it?"

FLIGHT SCHOOL

You want to know what I did in the war? Well, I started out as a pilot but, unfortunately, I was shot down and put out of commission for a while. Then, on recovery, I found myself thrust into a teaching position back in England. See, at that point in the war, the allies were actually quite low on pilots, and so they set up various programmes to teach flightless birds how to fly bombers and the like. Now, don't get me wrong: I can see what they were thinking. In fact they told me."

"How hard can it be? They already have wings."

"I'm just worried there might be a bit of miscommunication, sir."

"Well, I'm sure you can handle it. I mean, we already taught the pigs and you know what they say about them."

"I guess…."

"Good." Officially called the Avian Aviation Division but later abbreviated to the A.A.D., I began with classes of thirty at a time of various species of flightless fowl and the odd slow learning pig.

"Okay, okay - calm down. Calm down. You're not here to make friends. Now, does anybody have any previous experience or are you all as useless as you look? No? okay, then. From the top: this is the Lockheed Hudson. It will take six of you bird brains to operate it efficiently. It has guns: two x 0.303 in (7.7 mm) Browning machine guns in the dorsal turret, 2 x .303 Browning machine guns in the nose, and will hold 750 lb (340 kg) of bombs or depth charges. Now, then - any questions, or shall I continue?" I would say this and, without fail, be answered with, "What's a bomb?"

Now, see, when I say 'without fail', it was only after practice that I knew what they would ask. Thusly, the first time, I was taken aback at such a question when a rather annoying duck who had lost his actual wings spoke up.

"What's a bomb?"

"Sorry, what?

"Oh, are you not English? Sorry. I will talk slower. W-O-T-TI-S-AB-O-U-M-B?"

"Erm.. it's something we drop from the bottom of the plane?"

"Like an egg?"

"Yes exactly, like an egg."

"So, you drop your babies from this plane thing, then what?"

"Well, when the bombs land on their target they explode, destroying...wait. No, it's only like an egg because it drops from the bottom of the plane."

"So, it doesn't hatch?"

"No, it doesn't hatch. It explodes."

"With babies?"

"No! There are no babies!"

"But you said it's like an egg."

"Look, forget the egg. Think of it more like faeces."

"What are faeces?"

"The white stuff that falls out of you."

"Oh, so the bombs have shit in them?"

"Yes. The bombs have shit in them. Some very serious shit. Do you understand now?"

"Yeah, I think so. These planes have bombs in them full of shit that we drop on people?"

"Yes. Now, moving on, if that's all sorted?" I said, climbing down from my wit's end. But apparently, we were not done with my best student.

"I have another question."

"Okay. Yes?"

"How does it fly?"

"How does it fly?"

"Yeah. How does it fly? Now, don't get me wrong - I know the reason we are here is to learn how to fly but, from my point of view, it looks a bit hard."

"Well, we have barely started, after all. I'm sure once you get going, you will take to it like a duck to water."

"I can't swim either."

"Oh, sorry."

"That's okay. You didn't know, and that's not what I meant. I mean it's just hard. Where are all its feathers?"

"It doesn't have any."

"So, it's naked?" he said, emphasizing the naked in a way that made me quite uneasy.

"Well, no. It can't be naked. It's an inanimate object."

"What's an inanimate object?"

"Look, if this is going to keep on going, would you like me to get you a dictionary?"

"What's a dictionary?"

"Okay, moving on."

NEW HOUSE

"Good morning. W. Wood Property Management. How may I help you today?"

"Hello, Mrs Tree, Velma Tree here, I would like to sell my house."

"Erm, did we not just sell you your house?"

"Yes, but you did not tell me I would be living next to a chimp."

"I don't see how that's a problem."

"You don't see how that's a problem? His bathroom window faces my bathroom window."

"Does he walk around naked?"

"If only that was the problem, the world would be a better place for it. Lest you forget, my husband and I are both nudists."

"Oh, I recall that quite clearly. How is he, by the way? Carpets still match the drapes? Oh, and he put his back out picking up your glasses if I recall - how is it now?"

"No, unfortunately he has gone grey with the stress of the house, and better, thank you."

"Good to hear. So, if that's not the problem, what exactly is?"

"Well, generally on a morning I like to open my window to let some fresh air in, and it just so happens my dear neighbour happens to use the toilet around that time."

"Oh, I see."

"Really? Because I can't. He knocked my bloody glasses off."

ONE PLEASE

Working security as I do, you come across all sorts. I recall I was working one summer at a cinema when this mum shows up to watch *Rats of the Caribbean*. Now, this was when the film was at the peak of its popularity. We were all on edge for people trying to sneak in recording equipment, so we had implemented bag checks.

"Random bag check." I said to her.

"Certainly. Here you go."

"Yeah, looks okay."

"Thanks. Here is my ticket."

"Wait - what's in the pouch?"

"What pouch?"

"Don't play stupid, that one on your front."

"Oh, that. Just my new-born sleeping." At this, the red flags in my head waved furiously.

"If that's the case, you won't mind me having a look?"

"Well, any other time, but I just got him to sleep."

"I insist."

"I resist."

"If I must, I will get a marsupial member of staff over here."

"I'm telling you; I don't have anything in there."

"What happened to your new-born?"

"Oh, shit. He escaped. Help me look?"

"Fine. Can I get Julie over here, please!"

"Sup, what's the problem, dude?"

"Can you empty this pouch for us, Julie?"

"Can do, dude."

"You can't. You don't even have a search warrant!"

"Stop. You are making a fool of yourself. Find anything Julie?"

"I think so. It's long and hard. I'm pulling it out now, dude."

"A tripod! I bloody knew it! Julie, keep going till you find the camera. I'm going to call the police and tell them we apprehended someone trying to pirate *Rats of the Caribbean*."

"Aye, Aye. my dude!"

DANCER

I make my way to the stage, everyone watching me as I weave across the floor. I climb up the stairs and make my way to the pole and wrap myself around it, writhing up and down. With all the eyes in the room on me, on my flawless skin, I begin to take it off as I dance, starting at my top and working my way down. The cheers begin and money is thrown onto the stage as my skin falls off and lands on the growing pile. Another layer shed at the Seductive Serpent.

SECRET

"One into town, please."

"Two fifty, please, sir."

"Hang on - how do you drive the bus with no arms?"

"Shhhhsss I have a good thing going here."

SUICIDE?

The most memorable case I have worked? Well, I would say one I had in the middle of last year because of a number of factors. I remember it quite well actually, having just got a new partner after my last one retired. On arrival things seemed like any other suicide: grieving spouse, offer of cups of tea and coffee, a dead body etc. Bill (my new partner) being the first to arrive, he talked to the wife while I finished up a meeting regarding a personal matter in the family, then Bill filled me in.

"Bill."

"William."

"What do we have?"

"Death by hanging. He's in the shed."

"Where is it? Through the back?"

"Yeah. You want a coffee? Tea? The wife went next door to get some as she was out, but I can get the cups out and boil the kettle till she gets back."

"Nah, I'm good. I don't suppose there's any milk, though?"

"No. Apparently the husband was lactose intolerant. I asked before you got here."

"Good thinking." After putting on the kettle and getting the cups out, Bill showed me through to the back of the house and down the garden. On opening the shed, however, things went iffy fast.

"Big Randy... no."

"I beg your pardon sir?"

I said, "He's a snake. You didn't say he was a snake, Bill."

"I didn't think that was important."

"He was so hung."

"What?"

"From the ceiling, He was hung from the ceiling."

"Yes, sir I can see that."

"Have you ever tried to hang yourself with no arms, Bill?"

"I don't have arms?"

"You know what I mean. It would be equally as hard for us, if not more so, to hang ourselves. So how did Big Randy manage it?"

"My Dog! That means he was murdered. Would explain the handwritten note, as well."

"There's a note?"

"Yep. It's in the kitchen."

"Well, what did it say?

"Like in life, in death, I will shed. B.R"

"Oddly poetic. What did his wife say he did for a living?"

"He drove buses."

"Really? Don't see many sexy bus drivers."

"Sexy bus drivers Sir?"

"That's not important, the real question is how did Big Randy reach the pedals? Actually, how did he turn the wheel? No, no, no - not important. Where has his wife got to?"

"Sorry, Sir, but who's Big Randy?"

"For Dog's sakes, Bill, a man has been killed. Start paying attention and stop asking stupid questions."

"Sorry Sir."

"That's okay, Now tell me again, where did Big Randy's wife go?"

"She said she was going next door to the shop. She really should be back by now."

"Unless she never planned on coming back."

"Sir, I just remembered there isn't a shop next door. In fact, the closest thing would probably be the strip club."

"Well, I wouldn't know anything about that sort of thing."

TURTOISE

It was Christmas Day and my mother had just died. Feeling the need to get out of the house, I went for a drink by myself. I was conflicted about things and wanted to be alone. I was drinking my second pint when a stranger approached me.

"Hey, mate. How are you?"

"Fine. Just having a pint. Is there something I can help you with?"

"Er, yeah. My mate and I have a bit of a wager on what you are. Are you a turtle or a tortoise?"

"What am I? I'm a Turtoise. Happy?"

"Oh, so you are like a cross breed. That's so cool. Are you a turtle on your mother's or father's side? My step-dad's a sea turtle."

"What are you on about? I'm half-tortoise, half-turkey. Can't you tell by my fine plumage?"

At that, the man apologized and left me to my drink.

On arriving home, I discovered some of my mother's leftovers on a plate for me. A mum to the end, I thought. She liked to make sure we never went hungry.

SURGERY

I get requests to perform all sorts of operations, from the mundane to the extraordinary, to the ethically questionable, to the just questionable. Example?

Last summer I had a camel walk in for a consultation regarding her humps. Figuring it for easy cash, I saw them that afternoon for the meeting.

"So, my receptionist says you would like to have surgery on the humps. Would you care to elaborate on what you would like us to do?"

"Okay. I was wondering if you could move them for me?"

"Are you sure you don't mean 'remove'?"

"Nope. It's for my husband. See, at the moment he can't reach them without a ladder."

"Right. So, where exactly did you want me to put them?"

"I was thinking on the front like your receptionist, ease of access and all."

"I see. You will have to let me think about this and maybe perform a scan or two. I must say, I have never had such an opportunity before. Usually camels want their humps bigger or smaller, or just removed completely, or there was that one who just wanted me to install a tap."

"Oh, that sounds good. Can I have that as well?"

That decided, I showed the couple a selection of taps. Opting for brass we arranged to do the surgery the following month. Making a splendid recovery she even sent me flowers saying how happy she and her husband were. He was especially pleased as it reduced his monthly bill from Yorkshire Water as well.

SOCIAL LIVES

I go for walks every night. I don't even enjoy them, but it gets me out the house, and that's my only motivation - to not seem like the shut-in I am.

Every now and then, though, I will see someone I know, someone from school, someone from somewhere and sometimes, somehow we get talking, never a honest conversation. They are not my friends. It's not like I have friends.

I call in at the fish and chips shop sometimes. They don't even talk to me anymore. I always get the same. It started as an excuse so I didn't just get my own food and eat at home, a way to maybe start a conversation that never worked, and now it's part of my week. Another wordless interaction.

I get home with my food and hope someone has broken in, waiting to tie me up and drown me in the river. I leave my door open as an invite. No one accepts. I can't even kill myself without someone else. Don't get me wrong, I tried. I spent a week jumping off a tower block but I kept landing on my feet. I tried to overdose as well, but them childproof locks are a bugger to open, and don't get me started on drowning. I thought I was going to choke to death the other day but then a dog barked, startling me.

My parents don't even call anymore. Then again, they may be dead for all I know. Would be just my luck. I must have nearly died nine times by accident, but when I really want to it's a no go.

I got a new postwoman the other week. She said her name was Jess. I asked her what happened to Patrick. I think I upset her. I close the door but hear the letterbox, only to find she has put a dead bird through. What does this mean?

It means nothing. She puts dead birds in everyone's letterboxes, of course. I'm not special.

I get a phone call the next day asking if I want to buy life insurance. I hung up. I was thinking of adopting a dog, but the animal shelter won't let me and suggested I call the Samaritans. I say no and they call the police to my location. I run for it and am chased all night. Eventually, I get around a corner and start acting inconspicuous by licking my arsehole.

'Smooth criminal' plays through my head as they pass by, none the wiser. Maybe I should become a thief, a cat burglar, I think to myself. I don't.

I go home and watch the news. The world's a crazy place, and I'm not sure I like that about it. Maybe I should become an astronaut. They let a dog go into space. How hard could it be? And it would get me out the house. I decide to ring NASA in the morning. They say they are not taking any applications at the moment: try SpaceX.

I go out for another walk. I figure I will try the library for something to do. I find a book about Egypt. It's boring. I find a book about France in French: I have drifted into the foreign language section. I go to the other side of the library and start afresh. I still don't find anything interesting.

On the way home I pass someone begging for change. I don't have any, but I find a dead bird and take it to him. He says I can keep it. I ask him if he wants to come back with me to mine but he says he's more of a dog person.

FISHFAIR?

How did I find out where babies come from? I think I must have been about twelve when it first occurred to me to ask. We had just started school again after summer and everyone was talking about having new little brothers and sisters so I asked my dad.

"Dad, where do babies come from?"

"Well, son, when a man and a woman love each other and they have been courting for a while, they can rent a caravan and head off to the coast for the weekend. Following so far?"

"Yes..."

"Good. Now, once they get there and have paid for their lot at the caravan site, they can partake in a special activity. First, though, they must take out a mortgage on their house. Then, and only then, they can head to the Fishfair."

"Hang on - what the hell is a Fishfair?"

"Well, if you didn't interrupt, you would know by now, wouldn't you?"

"Sorry."

"A Fishfair is a fair just like any other, except run by fish. That's why they're at the coast, see, and so instead of Hook a Duck, for example, they do Hook a Dog."

"Hook a Dog?"

"Yes, and if lady luck is on your side, you can win a new-born infant with breathing apparatus thrown in."

"What?"

"Well, that or a cuddly toy."

"But that doesn't answer my question. If you got me at a Fishfair, where do they get the babies?"

"No idea. Maybe you're a black market baby, maybe?"

"Oh."

"Yes?"

"So you won me at a Fishfair in Scarborough?

"No... that's why you're such a disappointment."

"Dad!"

"Just kidding. No one wanted you. We got you out of a bin."

VASECTOMY

Some days work is just hectic and some days I want to bash my head into a wall at how frustrated I get. And some days I self-medicate but that's not important. Example? One day, in particular, I just wanted to walk out into traffic by lunch.

"So, tell me how can I help you today?" I said to my new patient.

"I would like the snip."

"Okay. Are you sure? Have you spoken to your partner about this, if applicable, yes?"

"No. And if she found out, she would probably castrate me."

"Okay, Mr Abbit. Lie down and take your trousers off," I said. Something that soon loses its impact to hear when you have seen as many naked males and dodgy tailers as I have.

"I'm not wearing any. I'm just hairy."

At that my new nurse barged in - quite literally in fact, as she was a rhino. Don't worry, though: she had already broken the door bringing me a clipboard the previous week.

"Doctor, we have a problem."

"Now what?"

"We have a bird in room five and he wants to be circumcised."

"And you're fully capable of doing that."

"But it's impossible."

"Put your mind to it."

"But Doctor, birds don't have anything there to circumcise."

"Well how the hell would I know? I'm not an ornithologist. What do they have? Maybe we can improvise."

"A cloaca."

"What the hell's a cloaca? It sounds like a bloody instrument!"

"I think you're thinking of a clarinet, Doctor. And it's what birds have, Doctor."

"Really? Tell you what then, just cut it off and hope for the best. At the very least we can see if it works like a woodwind."

I KNOW A GUY

Dear Mr. Diary,
I have chlamydia. I don't know who I got it off or when. Maybe that seagull I met? I'm not too sure. That's not important, though, as I think the crew knows. I have started to notice them acting funny towards me: avoiding eye contact, stopping conversations when I fly onto the deck, deliberately avoiding sharing the bath with me it. So it begs the question: do they know?

Dear Mr. Diary,
I confronted first mate Rodgers today and it seems I was 'worried about nothing' as he put it. Apparently everybody on the ship has STDs, collecting them like commemorative stamps at every port. And as for the avoidance, they were merely getting ready for my birthday party.

Dear Mr. Diary,
First mate Rodgers got me a strange birthday card. It had the wrong name on it and everything! Well, so it seemed, until I confronted him about it. Apparently, it was for a doctor who helped him with a personal issue. Taking this as a, "He's okay if you don't want to have chlamydia," wink (well, I assumed he winked; he had his eye patch on), I took him up on it and booked an appointment.
　"So, you were given my card." The doctor said.
　"So, you were given my card."
　"Interesting."

"Interesting."

"I think I know what to do."

"I think I know what to do."

"Let me just get one thing from my desk."

"Let me just get one thing from my desk, arse."

"Pardon?"

"Pardon, stoptalkingass."

"Okay."

"Okayyoubloody ass. Finally listen can you help me, Doc? I have a terrible case of chlamydia."

"Chlamydia?"

"Chlamydia."

"Chlamydia?"

"Chlamydia, stop it!"

"Sorry. I just thought, you being a parrot and all, and the obvious issue we just went through, that you came here to work on your speech."

"Sorry, I just thought, you being a parrot and allshutup. Can you help me or not?"

"No. I'm not that sort of doctor."

"NO, I'm not that sort of doctor. Well, that was a wasted journey. First mate says you were a great doc, though. Really helped him with a personal issue."

"First mate Rodgers? Yes, he kept saying 'aye' and he found it embarrassing."

"He kept saying 'aye' and he found it embarrassing, ha ha. Really, was that it?"

"Oh, crap - doctor patient confidentiality. Don't tell anyone."

"Oh, crap - doctor patient confidentiality. Don't tell anyone. Help me with my chlamydia, then."

BIG SHOES

Ever since Patrick died, I feel I have been missing something from my life and, consequently, I stopped leaving the house and stopped killing birds. There was no point anymore, as I had no one to bring them home to. But then I realized maybe I could follow in Patrick's footsteps, so to speak, and that's why I became a postwoman. Now it's like I have hundreds of owners, and when I deliver them the post, I slip a dead bird through the letterbox, too.

NEW BAR

So, I went to this new bar the other day. It had such a unique atmosphere. From the ceiling to the floor was a deep rich brown, and balls of wool hung from the beams. The menu contained nothing but different cuts of raw exotic meats. They only served water, though, and there were huge cats lounging on every free surface. Do you know it? It's called Lion Bar.

TRAP

Unable to work the cow, they were left with one option.
So they sharpened their spears at the call to action.
The plan was simple - herd the beast.
Confine her till she revealed the secret to cheese.
Mouse Trap

TIS THE SEASON

Trying to sleep as I had work the next day, I looked up at my ceiling, eyes flickering on the edge of sleep. That's when the doorbell rang, immediately followed by an abomination of a rendition of 'Deck the Halls'.

"Caw caw-caw caw, caw caw caw caw."

I went to my window and shouted through the glass, "What the hell do you think you are playing at?"

Having had no apparent effect on them, I went to get my dressing gown to confront them at my door. Opening it up, I greeted them with, "Do you even know what time it is?"

"Tis the season, goodwill to all men."

"And birds."

"AND BIRDS!" the carollers said, all wanting to get a word in.

"IT'S ONLY NOVEMBER!" I replied.

"Is it?

"It gets earlier every year!"

"YEAH, WAS NOVEMBER LAST YEAR!" said the one at the back, only just counting the three birds.

"Whatever. Just shut the hell up or sod off. I have work in the morning."

"Give us a fiver."

"A tenner!"

"A BARITONE!"

"Shut up, Reg. A tenner."

Agreeing to their price just to get rid of them, I went to get my wallet.

"Fine, bloody cold calling Christmas carolling

crows," I muttered, and was just about to hand over the money when it occurred to me I don't have a doorbell. Unfortunately, voicing this revelation out loud to myself was a poor choice, as a black blur swept past me and off into the night, the rest of the murder following after. Well, apart from Reg, who was a bit behind the rest, shouting, "LEG IT!" to his friends, only to be replied to by the night and a voice on the wind:

"We have wings, Reg."

TRESPASSING

Our murderer was in great spirits after receiving the money, and wanted to go buy some whisky to celebrate. Setting off from the den, we wondered if we could just cut through the fields behind the street we just swindled and, if so, would it be faster? Full of confidence and bravado, we risked it and set off to try our new shortcut, deciding to walk for the exercise. When we got to the bushes separating us from the farmland, we took turns climbing over: Reg going first, then Ray and Rita, then lastly myself. I think, looking back, that's what saved me, my friends' caws warning me off going further, but I'm getting ahead of myself. Reg took the lead with great gusto after getting into the field, and started singing in a military marching style almost immediately, with Rita following second and finding it hilarious. Myself and Ray brought up the rear, cawing the tune sarcastically which ended up reducing us all to hysterics. Now usually, we would not dare trespass through a field as it was drilled into us as children not to, but upon finishing work for the night, and counting up our earnings on the roofs, we noticed this field had no scarecrow. So, after Reg stopped singing and we calmed down with our laughing, we soon got onto the topic of why not? Ray was somewhat on edge about it.

"I just don't get it, though. Every field is meant to have a scarecrow, Isn't it?"

"Well, I think it's exciting," Rita said, apparently thrilled by the idea. As for Reg, he just didn't seem to see the danger in anything, and me, I was forever the sceptic that scarecrows were even that bad.

"My dad said that a scarecrow punched my uncle Rob for flying too close to him," said Ray. "Then he pulled a feather out and stuffed himself with it so he could sense him if he came back."

"Don't be stupid," Rita said. "They're not alive. It's just this land is like a church or something. That's what all the food is for. It's an offering."

"Now that's stupid," Ray retorted, and that's when I first noticed the sound coming towards us - a large squishy footstep. I was about to ask if anyone else could hear it when Reg let out a caw, then he was gone in a streak of colour and honks.

Confused and startled, Rita went for the other side of the field, Ray following her, the two love birds still inseparable even in a panic. I followed shortly after, but we'd made the wrong decision as Rita and Ray were next, the streak returning from the side it had just vanished into. I realized it was using the bushes to hide its movement and it could have been anywhere. Turning in circles, I was sick with terror and on my last rotation I came face to face with it. But It wasn't a scarecrow, It never was. The Scareclown looked at me with his painted-on smile and coal black nose. He reeked of manure and my friends' blood, and wore a wig of feathers like a crown, Going to grab me, he shook me from my pause and I remembered I could fly so I shot up faster than the clown's arm and flew all night. My friend's bodies were never found and neither was the clown, but if you think trespassing can do no harm, remember that a stuffed dummy is just a dummy, but clowns are always scary.

SCARECLOWN

A wig of feathers
A coal black nose
Lips painted red with the blood of crows
Don't trespass in fields
Don't fly there alone
Don't fear the scarecrow
Because the Scareclown roams

WHAT IS LOVE?

"Alan, we need to talk."

"Okay, Sarah. What's the problem?"

"I have had enough. Tim can't keep scrounging off us like this. He is eating us out of house and home. He never clears up after himself and, frankly, I have never liked him."

"But he's my best friend. We have known each other all his life."

"Well, it's him or me, Alan. Pick."

"Just let me have a word with him, please? We're off out later to play Frisbee in the park."

"Typical. You two out at all hours on your 'walks', or going to play 'Frisbee', leaving me at home alone. I'm sick of it!"

"I could take you for a walk, if you like?"

"Excuse me?"

"Oh, sorry. Look, I will go find him now. He's usually at the park early anyhow."

"Sure... Whatever, Alan."

On arriving at the park, it didn't take me long to find Tim. He was predictable, as always. He was sitting, just staring up at the tree they found the postwoman up.

"Tim!" I shouted to get his attention.

"Alan, you're here early! Are you ready already? Oh. I got the Frisbee stuck and I couldn't get it down, Alan."

"That's okay, mate. These things happen. Listen, we need to have a talk about Sarah. She's not happy with us."

"Is it her time of the month? I thought I could smell something."

"No, and don't be disgusting. To be honest, it's our behaviour... she wants... to separate us. She wants you to go, Tim."

"Kill her."

"What? Tim, we can't do that. Hell, you shouldn't even say that."

"Kill her. I'll even help you. Why not? I kill rabbits all the time."

"That's different and you know it."

"Well, just sleep on it and get back to me later. Frisbee?"

So, we played Frisbee until it got dark, but my mind kept on circling back to what Tim had said.

"Kill her, I'll even help you."

"Why not? I kill rabbits all the time."

"Frisbee?"

On returning home that night, we found Sarah waiting up for us, steely eyed. She watched from the doorstep as me and Tim walked up the drive. Not wanting to continue our argument, I went straight to bed; Sarah joined me shortly after.

That night my subconscious was as subtle as a sledgehammer at a whack a mole. I dreamed of me and Tim taking turns throwing a Frisbee at Sarah's head, with Sarah running between us, trying to grab it like piggy in the middle. Tim, taking it too far, flung it with all his might, wedging it in her throat, collapsing her with a dull thud. It woke me from my dream. The next morning Tim woke me while Sarah was in the shower and said, "Alan, we need to talk."

"Okay, Tim. What's the problem?"

"I have had enough. Sarah can't keep scrounging off us like this. She is eating us out of house and home. She never clears up after me and, frankly, I have never liked her."

"But she's my wife? We have been married several years."

"Well, it's her or me, Alan. Pick."

"Just let me have a word with her, please? We are off out later to see her father at the care home."

"Typical. You two out at all hours on your 'Drives' or going to visit 'Father', leaving me at home alone. I'm sick of it!"

"I could take you for a drive if you like?"

"Really?!"

And so we did, using the time to make a pros and cons list.

But in my heart, I think I knew there was only one option. So, upon telling Tim my choice, we began in earnest and, true to his word, he helped me plot. In hindsight, we probably didn't need to buy the whiteboard, but Tim can be quite persuasive. The plan was simple: kill her dead. That was the hard part, according to Tim, as Sarah was a lot bigger than a rabbit and would probably fight back. So, on the next Saturday morning after her shower, we did it. I distracted her by asking if we had a left-handed bar of soap, while Tim sneaked up behind her, and then I pushed her over him and down the staircase. That didn't work, however, and only served to make her suspicious.

"Alan, the hell you playing at?" Sarah said, attempting to stand back up and thus panicking Tim into taking action. He lunged down after her, his whole bodyweight landing on her chest with an oomphy crack, and he proceeded to bite out her throat as Sarah let out a final bloody, gargled scream.

After a brew and a hosepipe shower, we got ourselves together and hatched up a way to get rid of the body. Thinking it best to cut her up, I went to get a saw and some plastic sheeting while Alan dug the hole. The next few days flew past and were actually quite fun, as our cleaning turned into a complete home makeover. I recall one day, specifically. As I was putting up our new floral curtains, Tim had to answer the door to a cold caller. On edge, I waited with bated breath to find out who it was and what they wanted, only to hear a muffled cry of pain and Tim shouting, "How dare you!"

Wondering what was going on, I popped my head around the corner to see Tim heading back my way, obviously angry. I asked Tim what happened.

"The nerve of some people. I swear to Dog if I ever see him again, I'm going to play fetch with his balls!"

"Tim, calm down. Just tell me what happened, okay?"

Letting out a sigh, he finally gave up his anger and said, "He asked me how much for the man in the window."

Shocked and appalled, I realized the reason for his confusion as when redecorating we had put some spiffy red light bulbs up in our front room. Explaining this to Tim, however, proved to be too little, too late, as he bit the man in the ankle for his remark and slammed the cat flap on him. None of that was important, though, as when we were done, we had upped the market value of our house sevenfold and disposed of Sarah's body.

Or so we thought.

"Alan, Alan - wake up! She's back, she's back!"

"What? Tim? What? What do you mean, 'She's back'?"

"She's back. She's in the living room behind the sofa!"

I stumbled downstairs to see what was going on and, lo and behold, there she was. Well, one of her legs anyway. Getting a grasp of the situation, I scolded Tim for it just being her leg, but at least she wasn't literally back. Not so sure how it got there and honestly not caring in the moment, I went back to bed to deal with it tomorrow. The next day, I woke up to Tim next to me in bed.

"Morning, Alan." he said, far too happy for my liking.

Awake again, I got out of bed and went downstairs to make sure I had not just had a nightmare. But there it was: Sarah's leg. Deciding to go put it in with the rest that night, I tried to get on with my day the best I could, but there was something nagging at me. That night, me and Tim set off to where we got rid of Sarah the first time, only to be greeted by a horrendous stench of piss. It turned out Tim had thought it was a great idea to mark his territory to scare off any animals that might want to dig up the grave. Honestly, I had heard stupider ideas from him, so after getting acclimatized, I helped Tim dig her up again. Throwing the leg in, and saying a prayer for good measure, we re-covered her and set off, after Tim had used the facilities once more. However, that was still not the end of it, as yet again that night Tim came to wake me up.

"Alan, Alan - wake up. Sarah's back again. She's in the living room again."

Jolting upright, I yelled out an obscenity in anger and reluctantly trundled back downstairs to find her leg back where it was the other night.

"Spooky," Tim said, poking his head into the room.

Annoyed at this point, I confronted Tim.

"Okay, enough is enough. What the hell is going on?"

Playing dumb, Tim responded, "What do you mean?"

"We have buried that same leg twice now and yet again it's hopped back here when I've gone to bed."

"Are you sure it's the same one? She did have two."

"Yes, I'm sure!"

"Maybe it's someone else's this time?"

"So, you're telling me a new, completely unrelated, dismembered leg is breaking into our house and hanging out in our living room?"

"Okay, you got me."

"It wasn't hard. I can count past two, you know. What the hell were you thinking?"

"I like legs. Sue me."

"Tim!" I snapped.

"I was jealous!"

"Jealous?"

"Yeah. Even now she's gone, she's all you seem to talk about! All you seem to think about is Sarah, this Sarah that. I mean, get over it. It's been, like, a year."

Putting myself in Tim's shoes, I realized I had gone on about her an awful lot and for Tim, these last couple of days must have seemed like months.

"But we killed her, like, a week ago."

"Really? Are you sure? It feels longer," Tim said sceptically.

"Look, this is pointless. Give me her leg and I will go bury it, and her, somewhere else."

"Okay. Keep it secret, keep it safe."

"Ha."

And so that weekend, I went to go move her again only to discover Tim had come and dug her up for me as a kind of apology. So I collected the pieces and put them together in the boot of my car, like a morbid jigsaw, to make sure I had everything, and set off to hide her somewhere Tim wouldn't be able to find her. On returning home after the weekend, I was in quite the good mood, knowing I could finally get a good night's sleep. Tim, however, was not as at ease.

"Alan, you're back. Where did you bury her? Anywhere nice? I hear the park's good this time of year."

"If I tell you then my whole weekend would have been a wasted journey."

"Oh, go on - I'll be your best friend."

"You are my best friend Tim. Hell, you're more than that, but I can't tell you. I know what you're like."

"But who's going to piss on her grave?" he argued.

"I will, if you just drop the subject. Look, I know you can't help it, but if this keeps on, we're going to get caught and the police will separate us just like what Sarah wanted to do, understand?"

"Oh, I hadn't thought of it like that," Tim said, looking devastated at the prospect.

I decided to tell him some good news, as while I was away, I picked up something and so I took a knee and asked if he would take my hand in marriage. Obviously overjoyed at the prospect, Tim could not control his excitement, jumping up and down, chanting, "MARRIED! MARRIED! MARRIED!" which just put a grin on my face.

Calming down for a second, he stopped and said, "Are you sure, Alan? You're not messing with me? Like that time you said we were off to Disneyland, but you took me to get a vasectomy instead."

"Yes, Tim, I'm sure. And if you like, we can even go to Disneyland on the honeymoon. After all, they say you should marry your best friend, and you're this man's best friend."

Coquettishly turning his head, Tim said, "Oh you!" and he may have even blushed, but I couldn't tell with all his facial hair.

Things finally looking up since the brutal murder and dismembering of my wife, I felt kind of frisky and so, in response, I did the same coquettish turn and said in my most alluring voice, "I think I'm in the mood for walkies."

COPE

The strangest thing that happened to me while working in the store? I would say it was that poor woman who was trying to stack the shelves. I remember it was about dinner time one day when I got the call. "Go stop a woman from stacking the shelves," my boss says to me. I headed down to the floor and found her about halfway up one of the refrigerated isles, clearly distressed, with eggs everywhere, clucking at anyone trying to get close. So I walked up to her slowly and, in my softest voice said, "Excuse me, Miss - are you okay? You seem to have gotten your eggs everywhere."

"Cluck off. You're just as bad as them sexy farmers."

"Okay, but I don't suppose you would like me to help pick them up first? You can't leave them here. After all, you might confuse the customers."

"I said cluck off!"

"I'm sorry but I don't think I can do that, and, from a moral standpoint, I don't believe you should be leaving your eggs here, or be left alone at the moment. Tell you what, why don't you come back to the office and have a cup of tea with me?"

This seemed to ruffle her even more.

"Why not? I made them myself. Are mine not good enough? It's not like it will cost the shop anything! And I prefer coffee!"

My attempt at a soft approach not working, I decided to try and keep her in the store until help could arrive.

"I'm sorry, but I'm going to have to keep you here for your own good. You are obviously not coping well with your situation."

That's when she started to throw eggs at me to mask her escape.

"No, I refuse. Take this! Yah! Cluck. Cluckcluck."

"Oh, Dear Dog, how could you?"

After clearing myself up and making a statement to the police I went back to work. Only to find out the next day that she left the rest of the eggs on some unwitting accomplice's doorstep, leaving them to figure it for a random act of kindness and make omelettes every day that week, as there was, like, a stupid amount of eggs. Like, if it had happened to me, I would have called the police. Also, on the subject of eggs, why are there them little lions on eggs? Do chickens lay lions? Do lions lay chickens? Which came first - the chicken or the lion? What is the government not telling us about eggs?"

HOSPITAL

I was finally going to get a little brother. My father even said I could come to the hospital with him instead of staying with a babysitter, as long as I behaved. After all, I knew what he went through just to get the licence to raise me free range.

On arriving at the hospital, my dad led us over to the reception desk to get directions. While standing there, waiting for him to finish, I felt something brush against my legs. On looking down to see what it was, though, I was just greeted by several ducks. I simply shook my head. They were probably quacks here to work, after all. Dad finished up with the receptionist, then dragged me to the maternity ward.

Nine hours later, I was bored out of my mind and thirsty. So I shook my dad down for some money for the vending machine and then set off to find one. Now, I will admit I'm not the best at directions, but hospitals are like mazes sometimes and I found myself lost in what I could only assume was the crystal-healing department as, yet again, there were the ducks. So I went up to them to see if they could point me the right direction. It turns out they were about to head that way themselves as they had just called at the canteen for bread first, because apparently what they did was hungry work. They led me back the correct way and took me directly to a vending machine, but seemed in a rush to leave when we got there.

The quacks finally gone, I found myself third in line to use the vending machine and so looked around while I was waiting. That was when I noticed it. Identical to a road sign, in fact. A circle with a big red border and a big red strike through a picture of a duck. Puzzled, I decided to ask my dad. Unfortunately, though, I quickly got lost again and ended up back at the hospital's reception. Somewhat embarrassed to ask for directions again at the tender age of 67, I reluctantly approached the receptionist for help, when all of a sudden the ducks came waddling past at great speed. With bibs on for some reason and one was even wearing a bra cup like a hat! They were swiftly followed by two security guards with nets. Now more curious than puzzled, I figured I would ask the receptionist what was happening.

"Excuse me, two things. One: could you direct me back to the maternity ward? And two: why are the security guards chasing them doctors?"

Replying with a smile the receptionist told me, "I sure can! As for your other question, we have a terrible problem with suckling ducks."

FIRED

Stood on the diving board, I looked down at Lewis taking his break. I knew what I had to do but it still felt like a dick move to fire him. He was perhaps the most qualified swimming instructor to ever teach here, but ultimately it had to be done.

"Lewis!" I shouted from on high to catch his attention and take him in all his blubbery glory.

"Hey, boss. What's up? Apart from you, of course," he said.

"You're fired," I said remorsefully.

"What? Speak up. I can't hear you all the way up there unless you shout."

Realizing my mistake, I shouted, repeating myself with more conviction.

"Lewis, I'm sorry to tell you this, but you're fired."

Letting it settle in, I stood on the diving board and waited for him to say something, to say anything. After all, it was my idea to hire him in the first place.

"Why?" he said, clearly saddened.

"Because no one else can fit in the bloody pool. You may be a great swimmer but your theory lessons are not helping anyone."

"I see," he responded before pausing briefly and then continuing. "Am I still okay to teach my karate lessons here on alternate weekends?"

Not aware of this arrangement, I said I would look into it for him.

I took it up later with management, (a lovely cobra called Kai). She told me she had, "Totally forgot about the lessons to be honest," and, "I was sceptical he would follow through with them when I agreed to it. And even if he did do them, how the hell does he expect anyone to flip him? He's a bloody whale!"

Wanting to honour his agreement, however, she said Lewis could go ahead with the lessons for as long as he liked, as she didn't expect anyone would take him up on his classes. Much to her chagrin however, Lewis had already lined up pupils by seducing his swimming students into taking up karate, through his theoretical classes on paddling and the usefulness of blowholes.

One year later, Lewis had a highly profitable dojo, the biggest in Western-Super-Mare. The swimming pool, however, had not seen a swimmer since Lewis's firing. Kai was not pleased though, and wanted revenge against Lewis and his treacherous students. Choosing to set up a rival school, she used the car park as her dojo and got to work recruiting students to take Lewis down. Kai's wife, however, had had enough of the "Stupid fucking karate whale," and left her, taking the kids to move in with her sister in a two-storey bungalow.

MESSAGE

So I was watching random stuff on YouTube the other day, earphones in, dead to the wider world, when I had to get up to pee. In the bathroom I unzipped and waited while making furtive glances at my toilet monitor (I use it when I'm expecting parcels so I know when to stop browsing the internet and get off the bowl). It was on one of these glances that I noticed a dead fish on my doorstep.

"The fuck," I said, distracted, and ended up peeing on my socks.

Having changed my socks, I went to where my camera interface is and rewound to before the fish arrived. It seemed he arrived by lift and was left in a bowl, and then jumped from the bowl to knock on my door and back to the bowl again. Missing just once, however, spelt his doom. As he missed the bowl and slid down the side to the path from my door. All was not lost at this point, though as he was soon joined by a stranger, but after some coarse words and refusing to help, the stranger stole his bowl and left him to die in the mid-afternoon heat. Saddened at this, I figured the least I could do was give him a proper burial. So I grabbed my spatula and made my way to my front door to scrape him up and bury him at sea... down my toilet. But, to my surprise, on opening the door the fish let out a dry, hopefully not last, word.

"Water."

At that, I rushed back through to my kitchen, grabbed a bowl and filled it. Then, almost tripping over my vacuum cleaner in my rush, made my way back and gently scraped him up and into the bowl. I left him a minute to recuperate and on returning he seemed in better spirits. (Which made me wonder how he would be if I put him into a bowl of vodka.) Thanking me for the bowl, he swam in what little space he had. And then said he had a message for me. I leant in attentively to receive every word as he asked if I had, "Heard the word of cod?"

Noticing for the first time he was wearing a tiny dog collar, I stood up and went back inside, slamming the door behind me.

"Bloody cold calling campaigning clergy cod!"

TAKEAWAY

It was a quiet shift in the takeaway when a cow and a chicken walked through my door. The chicken, full of energy, seemed to be leading the duo, despite the cow's more intimidating presence.

"Night, you two. What can I get you?" I asked the odd pair.

"Can I get a beef burger and chips?" the cow said.

"Can I get a half-pound chicken burger, twenty chicken nuggets and six pieces of fried chicken please?" the chicken said.

"Okay. Is that everything I can get you two?"

"Oh, and two cans of coke."

"Good call," the cow chimed in.

We didn't have coke, however - only Diet Pepsi. Not wanting that, the chicken said she would just get some milk on the way home looking at the cow for approval. The cow nodded and was okay with the Diet Pepsi. That out the way, I got on with their order, but then stopped out of curiosity to ask what was on my mind.

"Excuse me, you two. Do you mind if I ask you something? It's not often we get individuals looking to eat, well, *themselves*. What's the deal?"

The chicken, the livelier one of the two, responded before the cow could say her piece.

"We are what you might call animal cannibals," she said in a triumphant tone, waving her wings in front of herself in a gesticulating motion like one might do with one's hands. The cow however had different motives.

"Well she is, I just tagged along as I heard you were cooking Daisy tonight and I wanted to see that cheating cow got what she deserves!"

"Mavis, calm down," the chicken interjected like she thought Mavis might get angry.

"Sorry, Nat, It's just every time we played Monopoly…" Mavis said.

"I know," Nat said "I know."

JOBS

Working as a taxi driver has its ups and downs, pros and cons, and you end up with plenty of customers you hate and plenty you love. Well, not love but not hate. For the most part one fare starts like any other, almost verbatim.

"So, been busy tonight?"

"Yes, sir."

"What time do you get off? A late one?"

"Yep."

"So, what do you think of them Ubers?"

"Personally, I don't mind them."

"Wow, that's really forward-thinking of you."

"Well, see, a lot of folks have been put out of traditional jobs. Like, I knew this camel who used to work for the circus, but one day they told her they didn't need her anymore. They were replacing her with some gymnasts and a few more clowns for the car."

"Wow, that must have been a bummer."

"Yeah. She gave them the best years of her life, but anyhow, that's not the point. See, when she got the news, she handed her notice in and I suggested she become a taxi driver as she needed work. But she didn't have the brain for The Knowledge, see? She did have lots of experience giving rides round the ring, so she started doing that Uber."

"Ah, cool."

"Yeah. Don't get me wrong - there are people working any area they can get taking work off of taxi drivers, but they are also taking work from other

Uber drivers who happen to live in the area."

"Fascinating. Left up here. So, is this what you do full time? I know some of you make your own hours."

"Nah, I have another job out on the coast but it's quite a seasonal thing."

"Really? What sort of thing you do there?"

"The same sort of thing I do here."

"Really? So, what's it like giving donkey rides?"

"Excuse me?"

"I'm sorry - I just assumed."

"Well, you know what happens if you assume?"

"You make an ass-"

"No. You get out of my taxi and walk. Now get out. Shoo, shoo! Go on - get out!"

FAMILY FRIEND

Dear Diary,

As you already know, William rather magnanimously invited me round for Christmas dinner at the start of the month, as I had nowhere to go and I can get quite low in these dark winter days. Unfortunately, though, he neglected to mention that his new wife's family would be hosting this year and there had been a death in the family extremely recently. Almost immediately on arrival, I regretted accepting and after dinner more so, as I remembered how much of an arse William can be. Starting with a Simpsons reference, I could tell he was planning something but, I just tried to make sure he wasn't too offensive to his in-laws.

"Good food, good drink."

Thump. I punched him under the table.

"Hey, what was that for?"

"We are literally aiding in cannibalism and you decide to say grace like that?"

"Well, at least we are not committing it. She does look tasty, though."

"For the last time, I'm not eating your mother-in-law."

"But it was her last wish."

"She wasn't dying!"

"She was dying to be eaten." William retorted

"Screw you. You know full well her family was vegetarian before you married into it. They are only doing it for you."

"Nah, don't be stupid."

"They look up to you, you know? And what do you do with that respect? That trust? You eat their relatives!"

"Well, duh. Of course they look up to me. They look up to everyone - they're tiny!"

"Will you be serious for one second?"

"Dude, what do you want me to do? They literally handed me her on a plate."

"They don't have hands. Hell, they had to ask you to carve her up."

"You know what I mean. You're just being pedantic."

"You could have at least cried. Mourn, for goodness sake. A woman is dead!"

"No one else is crying."

"I don't think they can."

"They're not psychopaths!"

"I mean, do they even have tear ducts?"

"Huh, I never thought of that. Hang on - I will ask Siri. Siri do-"

Whack. I punched him again.

"Ow. What the hell was that for?"

"What was that? Are you two okay over there?" William's father-in-law said, beginning to take notice.

"Oh, yes, Mister T!"

"Okay, good. Would you like any more turkey, Andrew? It's what she would have wanted."

"No thank you, Mister T. I'm stuffed."

Taking advantage of my poor choice of words, William took the opportunity to slap me round the face.

"Andrew! How could you?" William said,

obviously enjoying himself.

"You're an ass, you know that, William?"

"That's PC William to you."

"Wait - is this because of the bacon sandwich?"

THE OFFICE

How did it go? Honestly, I'm not sure what I expected after I texted you. I was going in for a word. I just wish he hadn't been so laid back about it. It really put me off guard, you know? Anyhow, from the top. I was there doing work when I heard Bill walk up behind me.

"Knock, knock," he said.

"Oh, hey, Boss."

"Hey, Bill. I don't suppose I can have a word?"

"Erm, yeah. What's up?"

"In my office please, if that's okay?"

"Yeah, okay."

So naturally, I'm worried now, and that's when I texted you.

"Close the door," he said.

"Are you okay, Bill?" I said. "You're acting kind of funny?"

"Yes, Bill, I'm fine. I just have some bad news for you, is all."

"Oh."

"To get to the point, Bill, Bill has put in a request to be transferred."

"What, when?"

"After his back surgery last month."

Honestly surprised, I said, "If he put it in last month, how come I'm only just hearing about this now? I mean we have seen him since then, you know? He was at little Gwen's christening and our David's euthanasia."

"He says he didn't have the heart to tell you. He

says he's sorry, if that helps."

"But why?"

"He says you're just too big to ride him."

"But it was his idea we take it in turns. Being partners and all, he said it was only fair."

"Yes, I know. I approved it and I shouldn't have done, but he just can't take it anymore. In all honesty, you were considerably slower to get to incidents on the days that you were riding him."

"There has to be another way. What if we use a patrol car and I just run alongside? Or we can get a horsebox and put a siren on top?"

"All our cars are already in rotation with other officers, Bill."

"Well, what if I get my own, then? I know a panda who sells used cars?"

"It's too late for that, Bill. I signed off on the paperwork this morning."

"I see. So, where has he been sent?"

"The canine unit."

"What with that German? What's his name? Bill?"

"Yes, Bill. Hey did you know he used to be a shepherd?"

"Can we stick to the subject, please?"

"Sorry. Erm, of course this means you are being reassigned, as well."

"Where to? I always wanted to do undercover work."

"The SWAT team."

"The SWAT team? How the hell will I be any use to the SWAT team? I don't even have hands?"

"They said they need someone to kick in doors."

"I see."
"Bill?"
"Yes?"
"Are you okay?"
"Can I still accept bribes?"

LOST PROPERTY

"That was William with the weather, and now to an interview with our very own Bill Bridges and a representative of *W. Wood Property Management.*"

"Hi. Thanks for sitting down with us today, Donny."

"My pleasure. I just want to get these nasty rumours dealt with, like the rest of my colleagues."

"Great. So, Donny, let's start at the beginning with Mr. Pigeon."

"For the benefit of listeners at home, Mr. Pigeon has had his name altered for anonymity."

"Ah, Mr. Pigeon. Such a shame. I did tell him that the house needed work doing and was susceptible to damage from coastal winds before he thought about moving in."

"Yes, in fact he had that in writing and signed by you, in a letter, dated the fifth."

"See? I told you."

"Indeed. And with regards to the coastal winds, how do you explain the mentioning of them with such gusto? Pardon the pun."

"Whatever do you mean?"

"Well, after purchasing the house, Mr. Pigeon had a survey done by an independent contractor and he agreed with you about potential damage from winds of the coastal variety."

"And?"

"And he said that it would not be a problem since the properties were nowhere near the coast."

"Oh, really?"

"Yes, and the same applies for the other two in question, meaning coastal winds would be unlikely to reach any of the houses."

"Preposterous. I'm sure you have seen the properties by now. They have been utterly demolished by windiness."

"Well, two were. Strangely enough, the house made of brick was surprisingly undamaged, apart from a brick that had broken a window by the back door. I don't suppose you have any thoughts on that?"

"Well, clearly Mr. Pony followed my advice and made improvements to his house but cheaped out on the windows."

"For the benefit of listeners at home, Mr. Pony has had his name altered for anonymity."

"And as for the state of the bodies? Mr. Pigeon and Mr. Pike both had identical injuries to Mr. Pony, despite the damage being considerably less to Mr. Pony's house."

"For the benefit of listeners at home, Mr. Pike has had his name altered for anonymity."

"Well, what can I say? Sticks and stones will break your bones."

"Funny that, as according to the autopsy report, there was no sign of injury or trauma to the bodies via a blunt instrument, but multiple bite wounds from multiple sets of teeth of what appear to be large wolves."

"Shit."

"Donny, come quietly. We already have the rest of your pack in custody. To be honest, this interview was always an elaborate trap at the tax payers expense."

"Fine, I knew it, though, I bloody knew it. Why would you want to interview us in such a fashion in such a place? And you, everyone knows goats make up 90% of the police force. You don't even have a beard! Is it really that personal? You're only a pig in name, you know? Bloody meddling kids!"

"I will have you know I shaved it off to go undercover. I'm actually quite old. In fact, I'm graying. I have considered *Just For Men*, but I'm not sure if their animal testing included goats."

DISGRACED

Having already discovered a number of pyramoggs, Mack, the world renowned Sniffologist, followed his nose through the desert in hopes of finding something more, and he did - in the form of numerous catacombs and even moggified catavers. It wasn't until a second expedition years later, coming from the opposite direction, that Mack's boner was discovered and The Great Sphincter was renamed to The Great Sphinx. After that Mack continued working in disgrace. His reputation tarnished, he found himself an embarrassment to his whole breed. In confidence he took his worries to his priest who reassured Mack.

"After all, not everything that has been lost has been found." And he was right, there was still so much to be found, so many places to explore and adventures to have. With that in mind, Mack set upon every goose that came his way, wild or not, and chased them until one paid off. A chiselled stone tablet that had washed up off the Irish coast in 2004. Mack still had to translate it, though. Noticing similarities to hieroglyphs found in Egypt, Mack was initially sceptical it would lead to anything new though. Yet carbon dating showed the stone predated anything from his earlier work by magnitudes. So he persisted, and eventually Mack identified all the symbols on the stone to the point where it was legible to read.

Population density had reached its limit and so with great thought and trial we created a vessel to explore the sky in hopes of space in space. This action proved to be in error, however, as the shuttle crashed into a surface, the end of the sky. This was not expected though, as we were told of the stratosphere's great expanse in the tomes of our ancient explorers on expeditions to unknown lands and heights. Taking action now, our government has decided to use the great drill we used to mine to the earth's core for its energy. I am told the drill is set to penetrate the sky soon and I wait with great anticipation as to what we will find behind it. The heavens cry for our actions as we have doomed ourselves through our curiosity, as the sky held back an ocean, a world of water above our heads and now that the encompassing sphere has lost all its integrity. I am afraid we will all drown with our lives unfinished. So let it be known if this survives that curiosity killed Catlantiss, Meooow I hate baths.

Once Mack had finished reading the tablet, he placed it down on the edge of his desk. Then walked past it to go tell of his discovery, only to knock it to the ground to shatter on the floor of his office. When questioned whether he'd managed to read any of it before it's destruction, Mack simply said:

"I was barking up the wrong tree, it was just more about them Egyptian cats. The carbon dating was wrong."

MAKING A STAND

Having worked the milk floats all my life, it was a great disappointment when I was let go. But, being the sort of chap I am, I took it in my stride and decided to go solo. Yes, unheard of - but what can I say? I have a lot of spunk. Unable to afford a float of my own, I decided the next best thing was a stall. The only question then would be where to set up. Annoyed by supermarkets running smaller operations out of business and since I was the milk company, I decided to try my luck in one of their car parks.

THERAPY

Okay, but no names, got that? So, the most unprofessional I have been while at work? I would say it would be with a patient I started seeing last year. He was hated by nearly everyone he met on sight, to the point he wanted to kill himself. He found himself unable to go on living, and the fact that everyone seemed to want him dead as well didn't help. I must admit, it took me a while to tolerate him, it makes me feel absolutely horrible that I felt that way, the way everyone else felt about him. I recall our first session. I asked for my receptionist to send him in, unaware of his condition.

"Hello, Doctor, nice to meet you," he said on entering.

"Ahh! Kill it, kill it, yah!" I reacted on instinct and then proceeded to throw the biggest book in arm's reach at him. On realizing he was my two o'clock, I promptly apologised.

"Oh, dear Dog. I'm so, so sorry. It was a force of habit, I swear."

"That's okay. I'm used to it. Probably saves some time, to be honest. It was a perfect example of what I have to deal with every day."

"Every day, everywhere you go?"

'Yes, and I'm tired of it."

"I see, erm, let me just get a pen and paper to write some of this down. You startled me quite terribly just now."

"Sure. Just don't forget I'm here, okay?"

"Of course. Oops, dropped the pen. Let me just pick that up."

"No!" he yelled, lunging for me across the room, legs reaching out in panic, as I ducked below my desk to retrieve my pen.

"Ah, there it is. And sorry, no, what exactly? Ahh! Kill it, kill it," I yelled again. Having only taken my eye off him for a second, I found him closer than before and for the second time that day, I flung a book at him, causing him to retreat up the wall.

"Ah, sorry, force of habit... again. I didn't expect you to get out of your seat."

"Again, I'm used to it. Just getting here, I was nearly stamped on by eight different people on the bus."

"I see. Tell you what, since this was only a consultation, how about we cut the session short this week and let us book you in for next week? It would give me a chance to get used to the idea and maybe talk to a few colleagues and see if they have any ideas about what we may be able to do to help you, as even I have acted terribly today, and I would very much like to show you that we are not all like that."

He agreed and let himself out, arranging a session for the same time next week. Somewhat puzzled that I hadn't heard a commotion in the waiting room from my receptionist, I went out to ask him.

"Excuse me, Jerry. Can I have a word?"

"Yes, Doctor. Go on."

"About that patient - you didn't find him repulsive in any way, did you? Or maybe even, just for lack of a better word, scary?"

"No, perfectly normal to me. Then again, I'm half black widow on my mother's side."

NEW JOB

I went back home to visit family last summer, bumped into a friend of mine on the bus and caught up about what we were up to now. He mentioned another friend of ours (Samuel) and how he had just got a job in the fire brigade. Not believing it, I had to see for myself, so I got off the bus with him and we called up the local brigade about the postwoman. She had refused to get out of the tree for a week now, sustaining herself on birds she could kill. There was just one snag, however.

"I'm pretty sure that's only a thing in movies and on television," my friend said.

"Are you sure? I saw them get that cow out of the river that time, remember? That was hilarious, as the cow was having none of it."

"Yeah, tell you what, we could just set the tree on fire. At the very least the postwoman might come down if we try and smoke her out."

Deciding it was our best option to see Samuel at work, we rang first, then set fire to the tree, when we heard the siren to make sure we caused as little damage as possible.

"Look, there he is." I whispered.

Excited that our irresponsible idea worked, we watched from a bush as Samuel ran up, making the ground shake underfoot, with a thump, thump, thump, thump. Braking just short of our pathetic fire, he stopped making his siren sound, took in some water from the local duck pond (annoying a homeless shark), and then sprayed the tree with all his might.

"ELEPHANT SOUND EFFECT" He landed a direct hit on the postwoman.

"Shiiiit!" she screeched, as she flew several feet, only to land on her feet like nothing had happened then scurry away into the park, dropping several letters, understandably pissed off. Somewhat surprised, Samuel stumbled back and fell onto his end, nearly sitting on us both as we were still hidden in the bush. Now scared for our lives, we let out squeaks of pure terror, alerting Samuel to our presence. Having learnt a lesson and received an exhaustive telling off, we caught up with Samuel and went for a quick pint after he got off work. And a few nibbles of cheese.

SECURITY GUARD

"The strangest thing I have had to deal with? Erm, I would probably say the milkman. That was an interesting one. The guy was not even in the store."

"Can you tell me what about him was so strange?"

"Yeah, sure. I believe it was just me and Terry on call at the time when we heard that the milkman was trespassing again. Now, I had just got back from holiday and Terry was a new hire, so we were both clueless as to what they meant, but they asked for one of us go to the car park to deal with him. Intrigued, I went to see what was going on and, lo and behold, there was a dude selling his wares from a little stall. You know, like a stereotypical lemonade stand a kid might make? It was just like that but with milk. Anyhow, I go up to him as now it's apparent why he's trespassing. All the while he's accosting customers with his spiel:

- Hey, how about you buy your kids some nice fresh milk to go with them cookies?

- Hey, you look buff, I bet you need plenty of protein? How about you buy some of my milk?'

And last, but not, least the worst one:

- Hey there, I'm Billy, buy my milk. I made it myself!'

So anyhow, I try to get his attention over his shouting and eventually managed to get a word in.

"Sir, can you move along, please? You are on private property. My colleague has already talked to you about this before, so this is not your first warning, and I believe we made it clear we would be calling the police if you did not dismantle your milk stand and leave the area. Since this is the first time I myself have dealt with you, I'm going to be nice and not call them if you leave now and don't come back."

"And I told your colleague before, all I'm trying to do is show people that they don't have to be a cow slave all their lives as there are plenty of other, more deserving and great-tasting mammals out there."

"That may be the case, sir, but we have also received complaints about you from the customers - never mind that the so-called milk stand is a health and safety hazard, and the fact that male goats don't make milk."

HOME IMPROVEMENT

Yeah, so, basically what we do is, we go to a house and see what they want doing. Example, I had this one bird that wanted us to knock down a wall so she could put an extension on her nest. Of course, she didn't consider that her tree was adjacent to a church and it was not her wall to begin with. So then she asks for a basement, which again was a stupid idea as it would go through her foundation, you know the roots? Causing her whole tree to fall down. Now she's getting to the point of frustration as I have shot down everything she suggests. But that's when I had the bright idea to just put in a loft, and so we did. Unfortunately, however, we had to raise the roof of her nest, causing her to be more susceptible to lightning strikes as she still had a satellite dish so she could watch her favourite adverts.

LATE FOR WORK

"Do you really have to go to work today, honey?"

"You know as well as I do that my work is important in keeping scum off the streets."

"Oh, I suppose. I guess I will just have to keep your trousers warm for you until you get back. Actually, I should probably just use a hot water bottle, which would mean I could get on with housework."

SONAR DATING

Yeah, we had all sorts on the show over the years. A load of mingers really, if I'm honest. Oh, and there was that box of shredded wheat. He was okay but came off a bit dry. But as for a memorable episode? There's probably a couple, at least, from the early years. Oh, come to think of it there was the pilot which never even aired. That was an interesting one as we were still finding our footing.

"Now then, welcome to the show, I'm Cilla Noir and today on Sonar Dating we're helping Graham, an accountant in the sheets, but a hunting enthusiast on the streets."

"That's not a very nice thing to say. Never mind the fact I'm not an accountant. I run a model village themed around when global warming has driven everyone to houseboats. Also, what is that even implying? That, just because accountants have a somewhat dull stereotype, they're naff in bed? I will have you know, my brother is an accountant and he has several children, all of which are different species."

"Oh, lighten up, Graham. We're trying to film a TV show."

"Sorry."

"Now let's meet our romantic hopefuls, shall we? Before Graham goes off on one again. First up, why don't you introduce yourself, contestant number one?"

"Hi, I'm Ivan. I like to root through bins. I tend to exercise a lot, but not by choice, and I'm a natural redhead."

"Fascinating. Now, contestant number two, please introduce yourself."

"Hi, I'm Rover. I'm looking for a serious relationship but that does not mean I don't like playing games such as Frisbee, fetch or Cluedo. Oh, I also like rolling around in the mud."

"Wow, could be quite the catch there for Graham. And lastly, contestant number three, please tell us a bit about yourself."

"Hi, I'm Maddy. I work for a non-profit organisation. I like to sew, do jigsaws, and commit insurance fraud in my spare time."

"Me, too!" Graham interrupted, proving to me that he did not read his contract.

"Shut up Graham, you're not special. Everyone does! Now be a good boy and read the cards we gave you."

"Contestant number one, what would be your ideal meal to have together?"

"Well, to be honest, it would probably be whatever I could steal. But in an ideal world, I would say chicken. You can't go wrong with chicken."

"And contestant number two?"

"Erm, well, I'm quite fond of Pedigree Chum with a nice red wine."

"Okay and contest—"

Graham, still not getting it, interrupted again.

"Bad Graham. What do you think you're doing? Where on that card does it say ask contestant number three anything?"

"But if I don't ask—"

"If you don't play the game like we told you, we are going to be here all day. Now be a good boy and ask the next question."

"Contestant number two, I like to go hunting in my spare time and kill innocent creatures. Would you like to join me and, in exchange, where would you take me?"

"Ugh, yeah, duh. That sounds like totally spiffing. I love chasing things and it would give me an excuse to use my crossbow. As for in return, I would like to take you to the dog park. It's great fun as long as you don't mind that we're all nudists."

"And again to number one, would you come with me? And where would you like to take me?"

"Go with you? Hell, no! You know it took me a while but I remember you now. You're that prat who slit my dad's throat and kicked me in the goolies. I would recognise that voice anywhere. Who the hell organised this sick, disgusting TV show? And do I still get paid if I leave halfway through?"

At that, we called time as it was obviously not going well, then tried again with our spares and repairs contestants the next day. They were more on brand but trouble in a different way.

"Hi. I'm in no way related or affiliated with anyone of a similar name to Cilla Noir and welcome to the show. Sonar Dating is a show where we try to help one lucky hopeful find their romantic partner. So, let's meet them, eh?"

"Hi! I'm Comic Sans, I know I'm a bit of an eyesore to some but I have curves in all the right places. I like to be read aloud and insulted by people who take offence too easily."

"Disgusting. Now on to our contestants. Number

one, introduce yourself, please."

"Where am I?"

"Shut up and introduce yourself or I will flood your tunnels!"

"But I'm scared."

Frustrated by the unprofessional environment and unwilling contestants, I tried to move on.

"For Dog's sake, will someone talk some sense into the mole while we move on to contestant number two?"

At that, the runner simply shrugged, but apparently got an idea and ran off.

"Moving on. Contestant number two, where the hell are you? What happened to contestant number two?" I shouted to the cameraman only for him to point up to the rafters where contestant number two was hanging upside down asleep.

"Are you kidding me?" I snapped. "How the hell am I meant to run a show like this? We have not even got to contestant number three yet, and that relies on SeaWorld giving us permission to film! You know what, never mind. Do we have a ladder? I will get the git down myself."

At that point, the runner came running back in with a mallet and whacked the mole on the head, causing production to be shut down indefinitely, and the company to end up in court on kidnapping and assault charges.

Oh, and as it turned out, Comic Sans was actually Times New Roman in a wig. Apparently they were pulling some sort of prince and pauper deal but the truth came out when the police ran a scan on their typeface.

CHILDHOOD'S END

Wolfy

I lost all respect I had for my family as the evidence against them came up in court and I decided I needed to make my way over to the local pub for a contemplative pint. As expected, the place was dead apart from the Bah staff. After ordering a few, I sat there for a while, not wanting to go to my empty childhood home just yet, as I would be staying the night there alone before setting off in the morning.

Shep

Heading home to see the family, I decided to stop in at the local pub, only to find a mate with the same idea. Having not seen him in years, I thought it would be good to have a catch up with him and talk about old times. However, it quickly turned to a conversation of concern as we got onto the subject of the third of our old group.

"Wolfy! Long-time no see!" I shouted across the empty bar after recognizing his profile.

"Now then, Shep. Well, met. How have you been?" He turned and puffed, matching my volume and enthusiasm.

"So, so. Just back to see the family. I thought you moved away from the area, though. Became some big bad lawyer in the city?"

"Well, yeah, I did, but you know, family will follow you anywhere in name and reputation, so I'm back here, seeing what I can do for them. They got into some legal trouble with the estate agents."

"Wait, that was them who killed them pigs?"

"Well, I can't really talk about it, but their public story was that the houses were in disrepair."

"I see. Moving on, then - you seen owt of Woolly?"

"Honestly, no. I've not heard anything since I left the farm, but I can inquire when I get over there."

"Well, when are off over? I'll go with you," he said.

"Well, I was planning on getting a drink first, then popping straight there." I got a quick one in while he finished his and we headed over to my family farm, reminiscing on the way about our childhood antics.

"Hey, you remember that time Woolly got you in trouble for stealing your dad's paint?"

"Don't remind me! I was supposed to be keeping an eye out for them bloody ducks while my dad milked the cows. But Woolly tells me, 'Oh, it's December and I don't have any money so I don't suppose you could paint a Christmas jumper on me?' "

"Ha, yeah. Your dad was livid. Ended up shearing him as soon as he found out because you had ruined his wool."

"Yeah, and of course that's when he pulled the old sympathy card that he would freeze without it, so my dad ended up buying him a Christmas jumper, anyhow."

"Ha! He always was a manipulative little shit, wasn't he?"

To that, I merely nodded and gave a subdued, "Yeah," as I began to think about the lack of communication with Woolly ever since I left home and how strange it was.

On arriving at the family home, though, things seemed normal enough, apart from the odd blade of grass not where it should be. And my Rubik's Cube was placed on the roof for no apparent reason. Going up to the door, however, my heart filled with anticipation that something was amiss, and on knocking, I found the door primed to swing open for me. Turning to Wolfy, I let out a drawn out and whispered, "Shiiiiit".

I tip-toed into my parents' house but there was no sight or sound, no smell or trace or touch of them. Worried now, I went for my phone, only to remember that I never could get a connection on the farm, it being in the middle of nowhere. That only left the landline. Which was disconnected. Apparently, my family had been gone for quite a while and as for the Internet, the computer did not want to play ball as whenever I tied to navigate to my email a pop-up would come up directing me to dodgy knitting websites.

"This isn't good," I said to Wolfy, who was growling with rage at this point. Because my family had always treated him nicely.

That's when we were interrupted by a tractor's engine. Immediately suspicious and on edge, I grabbed a weapon and Wolfy got his claws ready. We had never owned a tractor you see, as we mainly dealt with livestock and hand-embroidered overalls. Rushing outside to find the vehicle, me and Wolfy both eased up at the sight of my father driving it up to the house.

"He looks terrible." Wolfy said. "Has he been ill?"

I didn't know. I held my hand up to get his attention and to show we were there. He appeared to not have his glasses on. Which was unusual for a man who always had them with him. But as the tractor drew closer it became apparent it was not my father behind the wheel but something in his skin.

"Shep! Wolfy! Long time no see!" a familiar voice rang out from my father's pale skin.

"Woolly?" I replied hesitantly.

"Of course. Who else? Do you like my jumper? I made it myself!"

Taking charge, Wolfy replied for the both of us. "Woolly, what's going on? Where are Shep's parents?"

"Wow, you need an eye test. I thought you lot had great eyesight but apparently not. Here - I have some glasses I don't need," Woolly said, handing him my father's glasses. Wolfy swiped them from his fleshy hand, cutting the skin below the wrist for us both to see Woolly operating it on the inside. This just annoyed him as he let out a Baa of annoyance, which was soon echoed from elsewhere on the farm. We looked around for the source, but this provided Woolly the opportunity to drive off, albeit slowly. We had more than him to worry about, though, as tens turned to hundreds of shambling, skin-wearing sheep. The whole village had been turned to skin suits, even the local Bah man. How did we not notice sooner? We ran for the road onto the farm, only for Wolfy to insist on holding them back, as the herd followed the trend and, unfortunately for us, they were dedicated followers of fashion. Wolfy said he would be able to catch up with me. I was reluctant, but seeing his logic, I told him I would get the car started and come back for him. However, when I got back to my car, the alarm was blaring. Shutting it off, I jumped over the bonnet, only to remember the driver's side was on the side I'd approached from. Awkwardly I made my way back around to the correct door. Inside I started up the engine but the car refused to move. I had been clamped.

Wolfy

I killed like twenty six sheep. Maybe more.

Shep

Somewhat back to myself after the confrontation with Woolly, I bemoaned the over-zealous parking warden.

"Fucking typical Ashley. He only does it to piss people off. He made more as the son of the butcher than this!"

I went on not realizing what it meant. And that Wolfy had made it back to me in more than one piece, as he was covered in the remains of at least twenty six of our attackers.

"I guess we need to find him now, then!" Wolfy said.

"No. I'm not going begging to him. I can just do it over the Internet when I get home."

"Eugh, you idiot!" said the clearly frustrated

Wolfy. "If he's giving out parking tickets, that means the sheep have not got to him yet."

Despite the revelation dropping, I almost did not agree to go find him out of childish hatred. But evidently our lollygagging had given the sheep enough time to catch up.

"Fine, where does he live?" I asked. I had no clue, unlike them people in small towns and the like, or in books or movies, who happen to know everyone and their business, and where they live, and their phone number, and if the local post office manager can't get it up.

"I don't know," Wolfy replied. And so we ran, going ever further into the village. We ruled out houses of acquaintances, shops and ditches as places he might be, and settled on trying the most obvious: the butcher's. A little bell chimed as we entered and a speaker in the corner of the ceiling played a recording of a television actor yelling 'Ashley!' to which he answered.

"Coming!"

It was evident he had lost some of the little sense he'd had when I had known him growing up.

"You and you," he said on entering the front of the store like a bad actor who had forgotten the name of their co-stars. "What do you want from me today, you fine individuals?"

I turned to Wolfy, concerned at Ashley's manner.

"Ashley, cut the crap and give us the key for the clamp," Wolfy said to the butcher/parking warden.

"Oh, so that's your car? Well, any vehicle that comes here never leaves." Taking the wheel, so to speak, I jumped in.

"Because you clamped it, you smarmy git!"

"Listen, Ashley, it's my car and I want the keys to the clamp right now or I swear to Dog I will use your own bloody knives on—"

At that, he pulled a curtain back and revealed himself to us, like a naff Wizard of Oz

"You're not sheep, are you?" he asked us.

"No, we are not sheep. Well, he might be one in wolf's clothing, but that's besides the point."

Relieved, Ashley straightened and greeted us properly. "Shep! Wolfy! You just got into town?"

"Yeah, we've been away. What the hell is going on?"

"It's the sheep. They have revolted."

"What do you mean 'revolted'?"

"Well, you've seen them, haven't you, walking around in skin suits?"

"Yeah, but it's one thing to have an uprising and another to skin family, friends and, to a lesser extent, local familiar faces around the village you grew up in."

"Look, I will fill you in, then give you the key to the clamp, but you have to take me with you, as I can't drive okay?"

"I guess, but you could have waited at the car and asked us."

"Well, I would have if that wasn't the most dangerous place to be, and all because of that Woolly bastard."

"Who? Woolly?"

"Yeah, that's what I just said! See, it all started when he went selling wool at discount rates under your father's nose. Taking it in bagfuls down all the lanes and even the wise man got in on it."

"I thought the wise man was wiser than to handle stolen goods?" Wolfy interrupted.

"Nah, just called him wise cos he saved big on his home insurance, didn't he? Anyhow, when he found out, he was furious at him and kicked him out. That's when the trouble started, as all the sheep walked out with him. All was quiet for longest a while. Your dad took up the violin and your mother took up the Rubik's Cube but they quickly became addicted. Your father decided that was a problem, so they started doing crosswords instead. But all that time, the sheep had become organized and had plotted revenge. They came back into the village, killed everyone and started wearing their flesh for all the wool stolen off them over the years."

Shocked, I asked him, "How did you know about the Rubik's Cube and the violin? And how did you survive for so long without them coming to get you?"

"I'm nosey, and I just turned the little sign round on the door that said I was closed."

"So, why did you turn it around again? Are you not worried they'll come get you, too?"

"How could you come into my store if it was closed?" I admitted he had a point. He continued to fill us in on the finer details, such as how long it took for it to happen and why he had not just run for it.

"I never learnt to run!" he said - not sheepishly, as that would have been inappropriate, so he shouted it instead. And so, after nicking a Zimmer frame from the local church as a sort of stabilizer, we spent the rest of the day behind the butcher's shop, teaching him the finer points of running for his life with us doing our best sheep impersonations. That sorted to the best of our abilities, we concluded as the sun set and made our way back into the shop to get some sleep for tomorrow's big escape.

Wolfy, however, had trouble sleeping and, admittedly, so did Ashley, curling up in the corner in a sleeping bag like a giant turd.

"What if they're at the car tomorrow?" Wolfy said to me.

"I don't know. I guess we will just have to keep running. They're only sheep, after all. How fast can they be?"

"Yeah, but there is a lot of them. They might block the road, or surprise us by jumping out of a tree or something."

"I doubt they can get up into a tree. They're not goats."

"Well, I didn't think Woolly could drive a tractor but what do you know? Evidently, he can."

"Look, this is not getting us anywhere. Let's just cross that bridge when we get to it."

"We're not goats either you know." Wolfy said with a grin, moonlight reflecting off his pointy teeth and, at that, I went to sleep.

Wolfy

After Shep had gone to sleep I was still unable to, so I made my way back outside to have a quick howl at the moon while I had a cigarette. A filthy habit, I know, but the stress was real. But as Shep's Dad would say, 'Enjoy the little things. You know, like hamster sumo matches, It's bloody hilarious!' And so with a smile on my face I headed back inside savouring the smoke and the memory.

Shep

The next morning, we woke up early to a second speaker nagging Ashley to get up for work. Fed up of it, I got up to kick Ashley awake so he could turn it off only for my foot to sink into a pile of something resembling a sleeping bag.

"Oh Dog! It's in my shoes!"

"Morning, Shep." Ashley greeted me from the doorway after overhearing my upset. "The toilet doesn't work. Sorry I forgot to tell you. My bad!"

I was tempted to strangle him, but I figured it was not the time and just flicked my foot at him, allowing specks to hit his clothes and face.

"I probably could have gone in the garden in hindsight," he admitted and handed me a cup of coffee. Wolfy, however, figured in for a penny, in for a pound, and decided to squat in the corner. We left him to it and went for breakfast.

"You know no one's going to believe us when we get out of here," I said to Ashley across the table.

"Well, I wouldn't believe it, either," he replied.

"Yeah, thing is, though, we don't know how far this has spread. For all we know, it's the whole nation - the whole world."

"Oh, don't be dramatic. If this was really global, don't you think you would already know about it? They're not exactly subtle and I'm sure the rest of the animals would be quite formidable. Can you imagine a sheep taking down a bear?"

"Well, I guess not. Then again, if it was a dark alley and the sheep had a knife, you never know."

"And where do you suppose the sheep got the knife from eh?"

"What makes you think a sheep can't have a knife?"

"And what makes you think the bear won't have a gun? If we're playing a game of purely hypotheticals, what's to stop a rabbit showing up with a nuke?"

"I'm not sure a rabbit could carry a nuke, to be honest."

"You know what I mean. Look, forget it. Your coffee is getting cold," he said, prompting me to take it out the freezer.

"Thanks, I hate warm coffee."

"No problem," he said as Wolfy finally joined us.

"You got any toilet roll?" he mumbled reluctantly.

"No, but I have some wool, if that will help? I used it to disguise myself when this all started, but they soon caught on to the fact that sheep aren't naturally purple."

Handing him a ball, Wolfy excused himself to clean up. Forgetting the topic, I drummed my fingers on the kitchen table and eyed up Ashley's knives.

"Ashley?" I said, with an obvious plea in my tone.

"Yes?" he replied, with an obvious unease in his.

"Can I fashion a rudimentary weapon from your butcher's cleaver and that broom handle?"

"I guess," he said. The relief passing over his face was all too apparent.

"Oh, my Dog. You have a sword, don't you!" I said, jumping to my feet. I realised if he did not care about me using his knives, he must have something even better.

"Nah, ah, no, I don't," he replied shaking his head. "What would I want with a sword? It's not like I have a dragon to slay, or an Orc army to stop from pillaging the village."

"Yeah, that would be stupid," I said. "It's a bloody axe isn't it?"

Admitting defeat, he let out a *shit* (no, not like that).

"Shit, you got me. Yes, I have an axe."

"It's a Lord of The Rings replica isn't it?"

"Maybe." Wolfy done, he returned and joined in the piss taking, as we took the mick out of Ashley.

"And my wheel clamp!"

"And my striped pinny!"

"And my fatty bacon!"

"And my lamb chops!" The mickey finally taken, we left it on a sour note. Then we got ready to leave the safety of the shop and go into the village.

All was quiet; it was weird to think there were sheep running around with my parents' faces and genitalia, but nearly as weird to think that they apparently wanted us dead, this uncanny sheep cult, and it all sprouted from our childhood friend.

"Look alert," Wolfy whispered, having smelt

something around the corner. Front of the pack with my back to the wall of the local newsagent, I took it upon myself to peek.

"Sheep, two of them," I said.

"What are we going to do?"

"I say you to take them on with your broom and your axe." Wolfy said with a small laugh.

"You can keep one back after all with the distance, and Ashley can menace the other."

"And what exactly are you going to do during all this?" Ashley inquired.

"Well, as the fastest and most agile, I'm going to go round to the other side of the alley, sneak up behind them, and rip their guts out with my teeth and claws."

Springing our plan into action was easier said than done, however, as the sheep appeared to not notice us despite our shouting and waving; until finally I jabbed one with my cleaver laden shaft, and it burst like a bubble.

"It's a trap!" Wolfy shouted, darting past the end of the alley, followed by numerous sheep. What we had mistaken for the real thing were just inflatables with a thick coat of wool to sell the illusion. Turning abruptly, we found were being crept up on - and with Wolfy off Dog knows where. We were left with one option: to head out the other end of the alley and hope there were no more sheep laying in ambush.

Wolfy

Not sure what to do, I just kept running. But slowly more sheep appeared behind me, leaping over garden fences and gates, shrubs and bushes and down from tree houses.

"They're bloody everywhere," I gasped. The longer they kept me running, the more tired I would get. Desperate, I headed home to my parents' house. Despite them being in custody, at least it was familiar. As for what I would do when I got there, I had had no bloody idea.

Shep and Ashley

We ran out of the alley, glanced about for sheep then headed off the way Wolfy went. We did not see the sheep for the trees - well, bushes - as they had painted themselves green to blend in, until a rather portly fellow jumped me.

"Hah, got you! You, Bah-," he began to speak before being clubbed away by Ashley and his axe. I say, 'clubbed' but to be honest, it was a lot more visceral. Because it seemed they had sent the lambs to the slaughter on this, or maybe they had just run out of adults. Either way, they peed everywhere and ran off, buying us some time from them, but not from the bigger bah-stards heading down the alley. And so we ran.

Wolfy

At home, it took all my strength to lock the door. They might not have been pigs, but there was strength in their numbers. In a panic, I checked the phone and found the cord had not been cut, an oversight no doubt, as Shep would have been the priority. But who to call? The Bill? No, they may be in on it. After all, goats might not be sheep but they seemed buddy-buddy enough. So who? And how the hell would I get them to believe me?

"The wolf who cried sheep -that's a new one."

Shep and Ashley

With the sheep following us I thought hard about where Wolfy would have gone. It was obvious really his parents' house. But apparently he was followed by quite a number. Luckily, we had a lead on our own pursuers: there was no one to cry wolf at our appearance, but it would not last long. Meanwhile, Ashley was getting anxious. And that's when I saw it.

"Roller blades," I whispered, Ashley looked at me like I had gone mad.

"No, wait - a combine harvester. I always get them two confused,"

Wolfy

I elected to call the army, although I was not sure what they would think. But, following my logic about my supposed situation, they agreed to have a bird fly over and do surveillance. Thanking them profusely, I regained some composure - until I heard the commotion outside. I went to look through the ground floor window but, the wider world was blocked by sheep - until they got ripped up and slaughtered by Shep.

"Shit, where the hell did they get- aghhh!" one shouted as more and more screamed and yelled. The ones closer to me got ever-redder with blood and guts. Watching on with fascination, I thought to myself that the army sure was fast, only for the last sheep to be cleared away by what appeared to be some sort of farm vehicle. Then, as I watched it go off back into the road to turn, I could finally see my rescuers as I made out one of my companions in this tragedy. And then the other, as he walked into view, before bending over and smashing in the head of a still bleating sheep.

"Now then mate!" Shep shouted. "I heard you had a sheep problem, but they all appear to be dead now. How's that for timing, eh?" He had a wide grin.

"Shit, is it good to see you. And you, Ashley. I thought I was buggered for a second there. I only went and called the army. Said they would do a flyover."

"Really? But then what? Ground forces?"

"I thought they cancelled that show?" Ashley chimed in. Not sure if he was serious however, we both ignored him.

"Well, they could, but even we don't know how widespread this is."

"So, what do you think they will do?"

"I don't know. All I do know is we should probably not be here to find out."

Shep

Agreeing on that, we all boarded the combine harvester and set off. We mowed down the sheep in our way but then the sheep dressed in flesh started to replace them.

"The inner circle," I pondered aloud, as we approached the roundabout near the farm and my car. We pulled up and disembarked. Ashley removed the clamp. That done, we got into my car as a low flying plane passed overhead but we set off anyway. As the village grew smaller in the mirror, we began to relax, - until a massive explosion blew the place up.

"Fucking Rabbits!" I shouted as the glass in the windows cracked and I lost control of the car, crashing into a hedge just past the road sign welcoming you to the village. We all opened our doors simultaneously and grouped on one side of the car.

"You two okay?" I asked.

"I am. Been worse, like. Ashley, how about you?" Wolfy asked.

"I've shit myself."

"Fantastic, nothing else then? Just the shit?"

"Just the shit," Ashley said in a small voice.

"Okay, then. Lucky for you, I have some clothes in the boot I didn't unpack earlier. Wolfy, be a mate and get him some new trousers while I scream into my haemorrhoid pillow."

Wolfy

I made my way to the boot only to find it already unlocked, with Woolly dead inside and a crowbar lodged in his head. Presumably the crash had launched it into our childhood friend's skull, hopefully killing his sick mind instantly. The clothes were still there, however. I pulled them out from under him and shut the boot. Choosing not to tell

Shep about our former friend's corpse in the back, I handed Ashley the spare clothes. As we set off I tried not to seem bothered, but it was hard. The last couple of days had taken a lot out of me. But I tried my hardest and maintained my hollowness for the rest of the trip to the nearest town. There I re-established connection with the army and filled them in on the madness that had unfolded. That done, I said my goodbyes to Shep and Ashley and had a moment of silence for Shep's parents, but only a moment as I had a dead sheep to dispose of. I suppose that's just how things are on coming back to a place you once called home: the people change, the animals change, the whole community changes, and you just have to act like things are normal, even though some things are just not like what they used to be.

POST

Why was I up the tree? Fine. You know what? I'm getting tired of the question anyhow. I was doing my route delivering post when I got to a street I hadn't delivered to before, being new on the job and all.

"Knock, knock"

"Who's there?"

"The post lady. I have a parcel for you."

"Oh, so sorry. Hang on a second. I've just got in and I need to get changed from work."

"I'm sure if you're dressed, it's perfectly acceptable to answer the door."

"Are you sure?"

"Yes."

"Really sure?"

"Yes, of course," I replied, somewhat frustrated now as I had to get on.

He opened the door.

"Meeeow! Argh. Oh dear. I'm sorry, love. I wasn't expecting a clown at this time of the morning."

"That's okay. As I say, I had just got in and I need to get changed still."

"I will try to prepare myself in future. I have never been too fond of clowns, see. Oh, before I forget - here, have a dead bird."

"Oh, nice one. I love dead birds. Have a nice day."

"You, too."

That having gone well, I figured the next house could only be better. So I knocked on the door dead bird in paw, ready and waiting."

"Hello," said a rather meek cat, on opening the door a sliver..

"Hi. Parcel for you, sir."

"What happened to Patrick?"

Now I don't really talk about Patrick much since his death, and hearing his name again shook me to the point I could not bear to look at him. So, I handed him his parcel and turned around, not saying another word. Then when he closed his door I slipped a dead bird into his letterbox. Things went as normal for a while – letter, dead bird, letter, dead bird, etc. - but then I got to the house that started the difficulties. I knocked hoping for a smoother time of it.

"Knock, knock."

"Put it on the doorstep!" a voice shouted from behind the door. I was tempted to do just that, so I checked the parcel for whether or not he had to sign for it. Luck was not on my side.

"Sir, you have to open up," I said. "I require your signature."

Slowly the door opened and out of the darkness crawled a spider, I bloody hate spiders. I threw the parcel at him and, not bothering with the signature, I legged it across the road and up the tallest tree I could find. I stayed there until the fire brigade was called. It was only on getting back to the depot a week later, I realised I had forgotten to give the spider his dead bird, so I crept back in the night with it and, as an apology, all the flies off of Patrick's old trousers as well. After all, neither snow nor rain nor heat nor gloom of spiders stays these couriers from the swift completion of their appointed rounds.

THERAPY SESSION TWO

Did he come back? Yes, he did, actually. Things were still not perfect, but I managed to get a few ideas on how to deal with him better from my colleagues.

"Hi. So how are you this week? Have things been any better?" I asked him.

"Okay, I guess. Erm, why are you looking at the wall?"

The patient had noticed my new tactic, so I figured I best address it. Not turning around, I said, "Well, I talked to my colleague last week after your session and we decided that me not looking at you would be worth a shot, as part of the problem is, well, your appearance."

"So you think it's just because I'm ugly? Do you plan on doing this the whole session? It's quite ominous."

Trying to reassure him, I put my hands together in a cradle of concern but in retrospect from behind it probably looked like I was about to pee. "Really? I'd say it was more... creepy. Besides, if it's not broke, don't fix it, and I think things are going quite splendidly at the moment, don't you?" I approached him backwards, before tripping over my waste paper basket.

"I guess. Couldn't I just phone you, though, if you are going to just look at the wall? I would save a ton on bus fare."

I looked up at the ceiling to avoid making eye contact and said, "No. of course not. Two words: exposure therapy. It will do us both good."

"Okay, then," he said with a hint of scepticism and anxiety, or he could have just needed the toilet. I'm terrible with tone of voice.

"So, moving on, why don't you tell me about your week in more detail. Any improvement?"

"Not really. Just the usual screaming, stomping, whacks, and glasses."

"I see. And how does that make you feel?"

"Pretty crappy."

"Interesting." I had suspected as much.

"Are you reading from a script?"

I checked my script. "No."

"Okay then. Oh, I just remembered - I did scare the post woman off."

"Really? Did you get your post?"

"Yes."

"Well, I don't see the problem then, as long as she does her job."

"I think she even came back later and put a dead bird through my letterbox."

"Huh okay, can't think why she would do that," I replied, genuinely curious and partially blind now from my rather bright light bulbs.

"I mean, she is a cat, but it's not like I own her or anything."

"Interesting. Odd behaviour, nonetheless."

"I know, right? I can't even get rid of it though, as it's too big for me to move and I'm not calling a cleaner again as last time they took down all my webs."

"Quite the predicament. How about your neighbours? Have you tried asking them?"

"Yeah, one wasn't in and the other is a clown."

"And?"

"I'm scared of clowns."

I tried not to let my delight show in my trousers at the cash cow that had presented itself - well *spider*. Oh! The money spider! I'm so smart.

"Ah, okay, then. Tell you what - I think I have an idea. Why don't you give me your address and I will ask my receptionist to pop by after work. He is half spider on his mother's side."

"Oh, really? That's fantastic. What sort? I don't suppose he has a sister, does he?"

"A black widow and no, I'm afraid not."

"Never mind then, dodged a bullet there."

SANTAS - PLURAL

When I was a child, my family never celebrated Christmas. So while all my friends were happily expectant about the holiday season, I grew bitter and resentful of my father, the gatekeeper of the festive fun. I chose not to ask why we didn't celebrate. I didn't want to face my father's ire, as even the suggestion of me bringing the season up brought a change in his demeanour. This was the case until I turned eighteen, when I decided to try my luck as an adult that Christmas Eve.

"Enough is enough, Father," I said. "I demand you tell me why we do not celebrate Christmas like all the others?"

The clock ticked for what seemed like forever until he said just one word.

"Ants"

"Excuse me?"

"It's time I told you, after all, so there you have it."

"Have what? Ants?"

"Yes, ants."

I probed further. "Okay, but could you please elaborate. What has Santa being ants have to do with why we don't celebrate Christmas?

"He's horrifying."

"So you're scared of a fictional being because he is horrifying?"

"Santa is real, though. I met him when I was a child and it changed me quite profoundly."

"Oh, come off it. Even I know that Santa is not

real."

"I'm not lying. Look me in the eyes and I will say it to your face."

"Well, if you really did meet the fabled colony, tell me about it."

"What proof could I possibly give you to make you believe me? You said yourself you don't think he's real."

"Okay, just tell me how you met Santa as you allegedly did and if I believe you, I will forgive you for your trauma."

"Okay, but if you believe me, you don't have to forgive me. All I want from you is one thing."

"What?"

"If you believe me, help me kill Santa once and for all. I have been trying for years by myself to no avail, but another pair of hands might just do it."

"Wait, you have been trying to kill Santa every year? That suggests he keeps coming back even with the attempts on his life."

"Yes. No matter what we did, the next year without fail, he would come back as if nothing ever happened."

"We?"

"Oh, yeah, sorry. Your mother knew as well. She helped until..."

"She died at Christmas. You said she passed in her sleep."

"I wanted to spare you from it. You were too young, too naive, to understand."

"Well, tell me now. Tell me about Santa. Tell me what about him makes him such a monster - apart from the fact he killed my mother."

"She died fighting him. There is a difference, and okay then, you're in if you believe me, though, yeah?"

"Yes. For goodness' sake, get on with it. Just don't start with the night before Christmas."

At that he nodded, and the night turned from a quick Christmas Eve visit to the longest night of my life as my father began to recount the tale of him staying up to see Santa.

"It was nearly midnight and I had stayed up, and I was glancing back and forth from the clock at the end of the landing to the stairs when I noticed the clock had stopped, the pendulum in mid-swing. Wondering when it had stopped, I decided to check the one downstairs to see if it was, in fact, already Christmas and I had missed my target. So, I made my way downstairs to check the other clock and maybe see the man I knew as Santa. On reaching the foot of the stairs, however, things were clearly not right. Everything was gone, was black, was nothing, yet still there. But not painted and not just draped in shadow. It had acquired a sort of coat. Moving forward I realised what it was as it retreated from my feet. Everything was covered in ants. Horrified, I walked on to see how far they went, every footstep causing a ripple of movement away from me only to fill the space behind me. Reaching the living room, I grasped for the door handle, ant bodies squashing in my palm, and opened the door."

At this point, he went quiet and asked for a glass of water, the story having an obvious impact on him mentally. On finishing it, he passed the glass back and forth between his hands, put it down, and continued.

"To say it was more of the same would be accurate, but at the same time it was apparent I had found something more than its parts: the epicentre, in the living room. The ants worked, climbing each other, forming two towers and meeting about waist height, then coalescing into a torso and sprouting two arms, a neck, and lastly a head. Not being done though, what can only be described as a jacket regurgitated from its chest, came out of itself and onto itself, followed by the rest of the traditional Santa garb on its head and legs. I looked on in horror as its swarming face looked at me, then decided I should say something. I began when the room screamed at me in a million, million voices in unison.

"'HO, HO, HO.'

"At that I dropped to my knees from the pain, the ants making room for me as they had not all become part of him apparently. After a minute or so I tried to stand up, only to drop again to the floor where a glass of water had shown up riding a column of ants. Taking it from them I downed it and thanked the mass. Apparently not having anything else to say after it hurt me, it offered me its... hand? Grabbing it, I got steadily to my feet and then everything went dark. Still conscious, I was moved in darkness until I felt a soft padding beneath me. I was back in bed. Still unable to see, I laid there wondering what my fate was when I felt the crawling of an ant enter my ear and I heard a tiny voice.

"'Stay in bed,' It said, now not in a nasty way as such, but a stern way, the voice of a parent. That's when my vision returned. Apparently, they had just completely covered my face. Going to scream after such horror, I opened my mouth wide to let in the required air only to be filled with ants and the return of the voice in my ear.

"'Quiet, sleep now.'

"I think either way I would have ended up asleep, whether I chose to scream or not, as, apparently, they choked me unconscious. Before I knew it, the morning had come. With no trace of ants, I took my night to be a dream and I sat up in bed still rattled. Hearing my parents already awake, I headed back downstairs to open my presents and settled into excitement and joy until I got to my last one, oddly smooth, clearly a cylinder of sorts like the ones we keep in the kitchen cupboards."

It was clear that recounting the events took their toll on him. My belief in Santa, whatever he may be, grew three times that day as well as my fear of him. On revealing this to my father, he gave me a faint smile and stood to his feet. Steadying himself, he placed an arm on my shoulder and said, "I never thought it would be you who would help me take the bastard down, but now that it's come to it, I don't think it should be anyone else."

After that, things moved swiftly, preparing the living room for the upcoming fight, covering it in oils and placing flammable sprays strategically in reach of our position. And so, with a presumed arrival of midnight at the earliest for Dog knows what reason, we filled out pockets with lighters while my father laid out the bait on the coffee table by the fireplace.

"One glass of milk with a mince pie and carrots,

check, check and check."

"Why is it on the picnic blanket?" I asked.

"Son, when you get to my age you will find it's the little things in life that bring you the most joy." With that being that, we got into positions and waited for the fight to begin. As time passed I began to think on things more. Surely it was nonsense and my father had lost his marbles. But then, at a quarter past midnight, he arrived. Just how my father had recalled him, he climbed into being in front of me after walking down the chimney. The rest of the room turned into a wriggling mass apart from two circles around where my father and I stood. My father gave no warning, springing from his cover and spraying him with ant killer. I followed suit only for Santa to begin speaking.

"Jonathan, how nice to see you again. This must be your boy." My father, being accustomed to the screech, stood his ground and kept spraying, while I, unfortunately, forgot about that part of the story, thinking it unlikely he would be in the talking mood after all these years, never mind jolly.

"My, my, he has grown up. Shame I never got to bring him anything. Then again, you wouldn't let me would you?"

"Shut up, shut up you bastard, acting as if nothing is wrong, as if you have not caused me pain. I despise you!" my father argued back, as I got to my feet and began my assault afresh.

"Good, good Norman, spray his ass to hell!"

Not entirely sure how to do that, I just kept going, getting closer and closer, and all the while the small bodies piled up underfoot until my father decided it was time to burn the Santas. (Santi, Santee?)

"Lighters, Norman, lighters now."

Doing as commanded, I set the closest pile on fire. The flame soon engulfed the room from two directions. We took our exit, grabbing my mother's urn from the dresser, and made our way to the front door.

"It's locked, Dad, it's locked. Why is it locked?"

"I didn't want him getting away, hell I didn't think we would get this far." Panicked, we turned to try and find the keys, or maybe use the back door, when we were confronted by Santa yet again. His small bodies popping and still burning, he reformed one last time, for one last act of kindness. He pushed us with an otherworldly strength through the door, bursting it in two, and onto the street outside before letting out one final scream.

"Hoooo ho."

I turned to my father to see his reaction that Santa ultimately was good (even if horrific), and was greeted by what could only be described as Santa.

"Shit! Dad, you're Santa. What the hell happened to you?"

To which I replied:

"Santa you're Santa. What the hell happened to me? I thought I was ants." As it transpired, I was now me, having killed myself. The role, having found itself in need of a replacement, picked me. Unluckily though, I was a lot less coordinated than the millions of tiny me's. I decided it best I not be found at the sight of a house fire and I and me called for the sleigh.

Having taken flight from the roof as the blaze reached it, the sleigh was currently circling the area, briefly silhouetting against the moon before it turned dramatically and plunged down to me. Getting in, I found everything rather instinctive as I had my knowledge already, despite me not being me anymore as I was still me, so when I grabbed the reins I found I had already had them, and I didn't want to let me drive. This was going to take some getting used to.

LAST WORDS

Dear Mother,

I'm sorry for my lack of communication of late as times have been hard. If you recall from my last letter, I was about to be evicted from my coastal home. Not sure what to do and down on my luck, I took to the local park until I was moved along by the police after the fire brigade reported me. From there I drifted, staying wherever I could find shelter legally, or illegally. Reluctant at first, I stayed in public places, spending days in swimming pools and my nights in the slides, feeding on what morsels visited me in my tubular bed. Eventually, though, I was recognised for never leaving the pool, and then an unfortunate and embarrassing accident was pinned on me. After a lengthy court battle (which I won by the way), I ended up no better off than when I started. Destitute again, and not sure where to go, I took a chance one night and leapt a fence into an empty pond. Seemingly unnoticed for a few days, I went about my business until eventually the landlord discovered my occupancy. Scared to talk to her I eventually worked up the courage, and put my best self out there. She called the police. They didn't do anything though but we did eventually come to an arrangement, as long as I could provide some sort of rent.

Now Margery, my new landlord, was nice enough but also quite fierce. Yet as the month drew towards its end and I was unable to even feed myself, I was not sure how to proceed with no resources and no skills. That's when lightning struck. Well, apparently it did, as I read about it in the local paper the next week.

"Police have revealed the identity of the local woman, whose body was discovered in her fishpond late last week as Margery Butter. According to family members, she was renting the pond to a down-and-out shark whom she had initially accused of trespassing in the pond in a phone call to the Police at the start of the month. The body of Mrs. Butter was discovered when her son, Lard Butter, went round to check on her the day after the shark's rent was due. There, he was greeted by the body of his mother. Worried she had been attacked by the shark, he went on to call the police who came and cordoned off the house until a proper autopsy and forensic investigation could be undertaken. The death of Mrs. Butter was ruled to be an accident. She had gone into the small pond to search for the shark and demand payment and an unfortunate and abrupt lightning strike electrocuted the pond killing her instantly."

Shaken by the news, and appalled by my own actions, I ran away. Hitchhiking my way towards London, I was towed behind any boats that would take me, then took shelter in London's many fountains (a great source of small change).

One day, our Trevor happened to walk by, having taken a job in the city last year, and he offered to take me in. I was unwilling at first; he, however, would not take no for an answer. The room was sparse to say the least, being only a fishbowl in his landlord's kitchen. I stayed for a couple of months, but I still felt guilty about Mrs. Butter and so I lied to him about finding a place back at the coast and left him for the North Sea. I suppose that's everything for now. I will write again when I can, as I know you worry.

Love you, Mum,
Your son Teeth.

WHEN I EAT MYSELF

Making my way back home, it was more of the same, as I kept panicking at not getting to fly the sleigh. I was constantly having to slap my prying hands away as I kept trying to steal the reins off myself and, every now and then, I succeeded - only for me to try again when I least suspected it. This sadly caused my flight path to be less than efficient as I skimmed the top of trees and burst through clouds. It was going to be a long night.

Eventually getting into some sort of rhythm, we decided on one of us staying in the sleigh while the other went down the chimney. Still being me, however, I couldn't make my mind up which of me had gone last time, as we both did, and didn't, do it. As with the sleigh, I was and wasn't doing everything one of me did or didn't do.

Sometime later, after emptying my magic sack, I began to head home and the rein tussle began again. I remember thinking I was going to have to work on this, and I agreed with me, but coming back over the ocean the weather took a turn for the worse. Lightning streaked down ever closer, then further away, then really bloody close. Eventually it grazed the sleigh, charring its red finish due to our inconsistent flying technique. Rattled, I grasped for the leashes again, ripping them from my hands and causing me to overcorrect and nosedive into the raging sea. Our tangled mess initially trod water, but

I had never bothered teaching the reindeer to swim, and so one by one, they found themselves dragged down. Their harnesses turned them into the antlered equivalent of each other's concrete shoes. Quite miffed at losing my ride, I turned to myself, who was equally annoyed. And I had every right to be: it was my fault after all. Putting my differences with myself aside, we figured our best option was to just start swimming, but just as soon as I started, something struck me as swiftly as the lightning struck the sleigh. Turning around to work out what on earth happened to me, I found myself alone, with me nowhere to be found. Alarmed, I turned in circles looking for me, until everything was fine.

With things looking up finally, I let my meal settle and got back on my way. My new body gliding through the water effortlessly, I started to make fantastic time. Before I knew it, I was home. Taking in the white plains of the North Pole, I let myself relax for the first time in what seemed like forever. After being murdered and eaten, I couldn't wait to get home. There was just one problem, though. I had gone from having millions of legs to four and, in my current state, having none at all. With no other options available to me, I settled in for one of my elves to find me. I used this time to contemplate my predicament. It would take some getting used to, but I was sure Mrs Claus would understand. Attempting to make myself more visible, I hoisted my new body up onto the ice. This proved to be a well-timed decision as an elf was striding my way, puffing on a cigarette (a terrible habit, but at least he wasn't in the workshop). I tried to flag him down but with little success. I attempted to talk.

"Oi, Bobby, stop skiving and get back to work!" Astonished that my voice was singular for once, I waited for a reply.

"Santa, is that you?"

"Yes, Bobby, it is me. Santa. I don't suppose you could go get help? I appear to be stuck."

"Stuck where? I don't even know where you are."

"I'm in the water."

"In the water? What are you doing in the wat..." His voice trailed off when he saw me propped up on the ice.

Giving him a wave of my fin and my biggest smile, I gestured for him to come over, but he was having none of it.

"Crap, Santa. What the hell happened to you? It is you, yeah? Not just an opportunistic shark?"

I told him about my eventful night, and he said he would go get some more elf power.

On arrival at the workshop I realized that word had spread fast, as Mrs Claus stormed out to welcome us back. She was clearly ticked off.

"Nick," she greeted me, then punched me in the face.

I considered eating her, but I liked her spirit so decided to see where she was going with it. That's when the diatribe began, eventually petering out into crying, then a soft sobbing. Then, gathering herself, she spoke.

"I can't believe you ate yourself."

The next day, I looked in the mirror. I had

changed quite a bit. For one, my shark body had seemingly grown a beard in the span of one night and had developed a healthy paunch. The paunch was more of a problem than the beard as now I couldn't stand still without rocking back and forth.

That's when a small knock drummed on my door and one of my elves came in. Greeting him with a toothy smile, I said, "Well, hello there, Peter. How are you this fine winter's morning?"

"Okay. Sorry to bother you," he stammered. "You need to come and see something," he told me, then he led me to the living room where Mrs Claus showed me the news. It appeared that when I ate myself, the whole world changed, possibly irreversibly. When I had eaten myself (Santa) becoming myself (Santa) making Santa a shark retroactively in the collective consciousness of the whole world. Personally, I didn't think it was much of an issue. I mean, they were fine with me being a colony of ants, before.

FAKE

I had waited in line all day and for what? A Santa with two legs in a terrible shark costume. Who did they think they were kidding? He wasn't even in a paddling pool or holding a glass of water. How on earth did they expect us to fall for this? My mother, however, had already paid for the "experience" and so I went at it full of salt.

"You're not the real Santa," I said, as I placed myself on his rocking back and began my smear campaign against the phoney.

"Yes, I am."

"Everyone knows Santa does not have legs."

"I'm eating them."

"And that's another thing, you couldn't get an actual Santa costume?"

"Look kid, I'm broke and I had it left from Halloween. What do you want from me?"

"I want individuals hired who fit the criteria is all, and not someone who plays on the stereotype of sharks eating people while also making money off them through a rather offensive caricature."

"Some of my best friends are sharks and they happen to like *Jaws*, it's a great film."

WITNESS

"Calling Mr. Henderson to the stand."

"Now Mr. Henderson, please can you tell the court what you do for a living?"

"I'm a Scareclown."

"A Scareclown. Fascinating! And that's why you were in the vicinity, yes?

"Correct."

"Now, in your line of work you deal with a lot of trespassers, so naturally you are all the more aware when a bird is acting in a suspicious manner, yes?"

"Yes, I would say so."

"So, seeing these birds as suspicious, can you recount the night from your perspective, from the point you began to follow the suspects?"

"Erm, well, I was just doing my rounds when I saw them on Farmer Pete's field. Now, me being contracted with Farmer Roy, I was not obligated to do anything, but being the professional I am I did decide to tail them and see what they were up to. On leaving the field the first thing they did was to make their way around the back of his house, which seemed especially odd when they came back around with a ladder."

"A ladder! And what exactly did they do with that ladder?"

"They put it up against the side of the house, directly under the farmer's bedroom window, then used it to enter the property."

"And from what you told the police this is when you believe the assault began, yes?"

"Yes, I believe so, as before I knew it, it was nothing but clucks, feathers and shouting erupting from the window and, frankly, it was such an abrupt commotion it nearly made me fall off the ladder."

"So, wait a moment, you were on the ladder by the window also?"

"Oh no, I got another one and put it against a tree so I could watch. I must say though it was the most vicious cockfighting I have ever seen."

"And you didn't intervene?"

"I didn't want to trespass."

"Yet you were perfectly happy watching him beat his meat?"

"Well in all fairness he does run a battery farm."

WHAT DO YOU THINK YOU ARE?

Last time on *What do you think you are?* we met Aiden. Aiden grew up in an oak tree just outside of Dalby Forest, but last week we discovered a shocking revelation that he was switched at birth.

"Aiden, are you okay?"

"Yeah, just give me a moment."

"Would you like to put some clothes on?"

"No, I'm not sure I'm ready for that."

"Please."

Having got him to put his penis away, we sat down with his fraudulent parents, an owl and a pigeon.

"Mr. Jones, did you ever wonder why Aiden was so different growing up?"

"I think we just put it down to crossbreeding at first. But as he grew up it was obvious he wasn't ours; our peckers in particular are quite different and he had no feathers."

"And did you ever look back on events and wonder when he might have been switched?"

"I think we did about fifty-seven or so years ago and we reckon it must have been on our holiday to Scarborough. We were in Morrison's adopting a pack of irregular eggs as we figured it was time we had children, when we walked into a couple and dropped the eggs. Looking back, I thought it was weird the egg had a breathing mask on, but we picked him up anyway and put him back in the box with the rest of the eggs. You know, on reconsideration, the strangest thing was inside it - what appeared to be a tiny bag."

"And what happened to the rest of the eggs?"

"Fried them."

"And when you discovered the truth, why didn't you tell Aiden?"

"Ultimately, he was happy and we didn't think he was ready for it."

"But then he went to school, correct?"

"Yeah."

And that's when things really changed for poor Aiden.

"So, can you give us an example of what they would say?"

"Aiden can't fly, he's got no wings, he is clearly a human child despite his parents being birds."

"And what would he do then?"

"Jump out of the window."

And so his hospital visits began and, as the years passed, he grew to hate his pink featherless body. The nature of his visits changed from healing his body to trying to make his body more like what he considered his birthright, having surgery to attach feathers, a beak, a cloaca and talons.

"Aiden, how do you feel about yourself since finding out the surgery was not necessary?"

Aiden made no comment during all this, though there was still the matter of finding the Jones' real child and so we began to research. After a few months, we tracked her down to a house in Scarborough, and so, after arranging a meeting, Aiden and the loving parents who raised him met up with Mr. and Mrs. Bagger and the Jones' real child Jennifer.

"Aiden, meet your real parents."

"Dear Dog, Aiden - you're magnificent. Look at his feathers, Amber! They look so soft. May I stroke you, son?"

"No."

But what happened to the Jones' child you ask? Don't worry, we exploited that reunion as well.

"So, as you have met your son, it's only fair the Jones' meet their daughter, so where the body? No wait that's not right is it."

"Upstairs. She may not be what you expect though. She's grown quite a bit since you last saw her."

We went upstairs to Jennifer's room and knocked, but her father came up and just opened the door, Inside we were greeted with what appeared to be an egg filling the entire room.

"She's still an egg."

"We figured it was a phase but when she never grew out of it, so we just accepted it. She is still our daughter, after all."

"When did she stop growing?"

"Stop? What do you mean stop? She has never stopped growing."

At that, we took our leave. Both families decided it best not to change the status quo but remained in contact. Aiden eventually went through surgery to reverse his bird transformation and got a job in the farming industry after his adoptive parents were found dead in a field. As for Jennifer, she kept growing and growing, eventually collapsing the Baggers' house and then overwhelming the street with her size and ultimately the whole of

Scarborough.

GLUE

I grew up in the country, on a small farm, never expecting anything to come easy to me but one day I was given a chance to prove myself.

As I was recruited for my natural ability, my step-father was obviously worried, after the many horror stories my mother had told him about sports injuries ruining people's lives. But I was naive. That was the sort of thing that happens to others, not me. Oh, how I wish I listened. This is my story, the glue that joins me together, that stopped me from going in so many other directions. This is my life.

Shortly after I was born, my birth father died and, after her period of mourning, my mother and the man next door got together. Both being widowed, they seemed drawn to each other. He was a kind step-father and an excellent replacement for the man I wish I could have known better. It was through him getting to know my mother that my little brother Milo was born - one of the best friends I ever had. I remember thinking when I first saw him, "That's what I look like."

But little did I know how different he actually was. It wasn't until a few years later that I started to notice the differences in our feet, our hair and stature, and the way he held himself. But then the day came when it was undeniable. We were nothing alike, and I was genetically superior.

Our other neighbour had just died and the new owners moved into his house surprisingly fast. Then one day, when we were out in the garden, they started a conversation over the fence with me and my brother as we were doing some lawn work.

"Helping out the help?" My new neighbour said.

"Excuse me?"

"What are you doing helping him tidy up?"

"He's my brother, we always help each other."

"Ha, you have to be kidding me. Your mother must have been desperate."

"I'm sorry, I don't know what you are on about."

"He is below you. He is nothing more than garbage to us and he will never amount to anything."

"Why would you be so mean?"

"Well, someone had to tell you. Go ask your mother. I bet she would not bring it up voluntarily."

"My mother died last year."

"Looks like she dodged a bullet then!"

"No... it went right through her head. It was quite messy actually."

"Really? Ha, that's amazing. Anyhow, I've had enough of this. Come along, Terrance, we have to go for our morning run. See you later. Brother - ha!"

And that was my introduction to the truth that the only real family I had left was different from me in a fundamental way, and that no matter what he did, he was doomed to mediocrity.

One day, a man came to our house. Apparently, he was there to see the neighbours Terrance and Dickhead but had got the wrong address. However, after his visit to the correct house he came by again and asked to see me. Confused, I asked him why. He said, he was a scout of sorts and he believed I had potential as he had seen me running in the field when he pulled up. Nervous about the opportunity that had just presented itself, I was hesitant to perform, worried I would not be able to stop concentrating on my feet. However, my brother said, "Tom, don't worry. You've got this. Just pretend that you're racing with me and forget everything else."

And so I ran, and the Scout watched my lap. He was quiet for a while and then broke into a grin and told me if I was interested, he could take me to the top, and that's how I came to know my manager, Markus.

This was my introduction to the world of professional sports and a few other professions, but that's getting ahead of ourselves, so let's hurry up and get there, yeah? I had been racing for over a year, stacking up victories at more and more prestigious races, gradually working my way to the top of the field. Everything was looking up for me but in my absence, things were not going so well for my brother. He fell in with bad sorts. I was none the wiser until the day of one of the biggest events in racing. Minutes before I had to run, I received a call. Milo had been caught smuggling drugs. My concentration shot, I shouldn't have run but I didn't realise how much the news had affected me until, at the last bend, I tripped, distracted by thoughts about what they might do to him in prison. Stumbling over myself I landed with my full weight on my leg snapping it with a loud crack. Lying on the track, my head was filled with anxiety about my conflicting priorities regarding Milo and myself. Then, thankfully, I passed out.

I went straight from the track to one of the top surgeons to look at my leg. I was in perhaps the worst agony of my life, yet all I could think about was my brother Milo. After the surgery, I was in recovery for a while, constantly waiting for news. I wasn't sure where they were keeping him or if he was already in jail, or worse, put down. And so, as days turned to weeks, I gradually tried to walk again, tentatively at first until I could do so unassisted, but it just wasn't the same. I could run at a pinch, I thought to myself, but I didn't think I could ever race again. My career was over, a brief but sort of bright, energy-saving light bulb. Depressed and not for the last time in my life, I considered my options for the future. If I couldn't race, what the hell could I do? That's when Markus popped by. He had an idea.

"Tommy, my man! How are the legs? How are the tranquillisers? How's the you?"

Not in the mood for his fake affability, I just looked at him.

"Oh Tom, why so glum, chum? Let me guess - you talked to the docs? No need to answer, they told me. Listen, all is not lost. I come bringing news of your brother."

At this, I finally paid some attention.

"Go on."

"He's just peachy. Got a slap on the hooves, is all, and a suspended sentence due to his history and the circumstances of the crime. He's back home now."

Shocked but relieved, I didn't care about myself anymore. My brother was okay, more than okay. He had his freedom - well, of a sort.

"And that's not all. I have quite the opportunity for you. How would you like to meet some ladies?"

Confused about the abrupt shift in conversation, but with my interest peaked, I told him to carry on.

"Go on then."

"Excellent. Listen, I have been having a few meetings and I think I may have found some work for you, and the best thing is you don't even have to be in tippy-top condition. Oh, and you get to pass on your experience, so to speak."

"Like how? I don't think I'm cut out to be a teacher," I replied.

He did not mean for me to become a teacher. In fact, if a teacher did what Markus wanted me to do, I don't think he would be a teacher for very long. Of course, I did not know that then and, being eager to get out of bed and back to work, I took the opportunity.

It was after about a week of "teaching" that I got to really thinking about my new job. Did I need my manager anymore? I may not have got here without him, but now I was a household name. Even though I could not race anymore, I still had selling power, and that was the marketing gimmick for getting me work, so the next morning, I went to see Markus to ask for my independence.

"You can't do this to me, Tommy. I made you what you are! You would be stuck on that farm without me, with your bloody druggy brother!"

"First of all, Milo has a name. It's Milo. And he is not a druggy! He was a drug mule, and he was forced into it, like you want to force me into giving you a cut of my literally hard-earned money."

"Well, you were okay with it yesterday."

"Well, times change, Markus. Goodbye."

"If you walk out those doors, Tommy, we are through, you know that, don't you? And you will never make it on your own."

It was no use as my mind was set anyway, and so I set off to start the next chapter of my life.

The next day I was eager to get to work, but I figured I should take a precaution first. So I popped to the bank and made a deposit that would hopefully get me some interest later. Then, calling in at the local shop, I bought a pack of extra medium condoms, some deodorant, mouthwash, Viagra and a bag of carrots. Going my own way was easier said than done, however.

Spotting my first mark, a strapping young lad at a bus stop in the rough part of town. I sneaked up behind him so as not to scare him off, and repeatedly nudged him with my head to get his attention.

"Stop it. I said stop it," he said as I kept prodding him with my head.

"Hey, I'm talking to you," I said. Causing him to finally turn around while letting out an irritated,

"Uhh, hang on. I have my earphones in."

"Hey, you, " I said.

"Arghhh!"

"Hey."

"You're a horse."

"Really? What gave it away? My long face or my

longer dick?"

"What?"

"What you doing?"

"Erm... wait-waiting for a bus."

"Cool, cool. So do you want to have some fun?"

"What?"

"Sex?"

"What!"

"Do you want to have sex with me?"

"But you're a horse?"

"Yes, we established that. Now yes or no? Do you want to pay me for sex?"

"So, you're a prostitute?"

"Neigh."

"But you just said...."

"The technical term is whorse. Emphasis on the horse."

"I don't want to continue this conversation."

"Whyever not?"

"One, I have no interest in paying you for any service you may offer, and two, I need to catch this bus."

"Oh, that's a shame. Where are you off to anyhow? Anywhere nice? Maybe you can ride me there. I don't check tickets, just IDs."

"Go away."

"There's no need to be so rude."

"Leave me alone."

"I was only asking."

"If I tell you, will you leave me alone?"

"Cross my hooves."

"I'm off to buy some glue."

"Why didn't you say you needed something

sticky earlier? There are two things horses are great for. Running and..."

"LALALALLALALALALA!"

"Glue...."

Dejected at my potential client running off, I was about to try the old woman coming out of the post office when I was halted by a horse riding a man.

"Excuse me, sir," he said.

"Well, hello there, gentlemen. Fancy a three-way?" I asked. "I must say, I like your uniforms, especially the pointy hats. You look like fancy jockeys!"

As it turned out, they were not fancy jockeys, and humans don't like sticking horsemeat in any of their orifices, especially the humans on duty.

Getting sent to prison really didn't hit me until I was standing in line to be checked in. I recall waiting there, hoof cuffed, watching the visitors' line, and noticing how they all walked funny like they had a bad case of haemorrhoids or something. Not to mention this one rat who looked like a little furry coffee table, and that wasn't even the strangest thing about him as he had a trail of what appeared to be videotape coming from his arse. While distracted by the rat-arsed little visitor I reached the front of the queue for the cavity search, but that's a whole other plot hole to fall into and you don't have a torch.

Welcome back. So anyhow, you get this idea in your head through like a cultural osmosis that you need to act a certain way when you get there. Turns out though, the biggest guy in there already had his eye on me, as not even a minute into our morning exercise, I was granted an audience with him and honestly, I hadn't expected him to be so nice. That's why I will never forget the first words he said to me.

"I wanna ride you all day."

Taken aback, I asked why I should let him have his way with me. And pointed out that normally people liked to use protection, to which he replied, "I can get you anything you want."

And he could. Who would have thought carrots were so easy to sneak into prison? I did notice there was a distinctive manure smell to them though, but I grew up around worse.

As it turned out, he had adequate protection as all he wanted to do was ride me around the yard at lunch and exercise breaks, shouting nonsense like "Charge!" and "Hi Ho Silver!" and "Ride to ruin and the world's ending!" (Which I think was the most confusing of the lot).

Thanks to this, my time in prison passed by rather quickly and I even met a few new friends. None of which in the shower unfortunately, as no matter how often or sexily I dropped the soap none of the inmates were interested in hot soapy passionate intercourse surrounded by hardened criminals. Eventually I gave up. My shower time was not entirely uneventful though, as cleaning myself one night after some horse play in the yard I was accosted mid wash.

"Rub a dub, dub, dub horse in the shower! Cleaning my Donkey my ass Mother Fuc-.. Ow!" Turning around, I discovered there was no one there. The rest of the prisoners had decied my constant advances and singing were not their cup of tea.

"Strange. Oh well." I continued.

"Washing my knackered knackers, I must be verry gentle! Since they earn me money and my income is unsta- Ow shit ow." Looking around again, this time I found my attacker - a hamster disguised as an old sponge, armed with a sewing needle.

"Can I help you?" I queried the wet rodent.

"Don't move so I can stab you again, see?"

"I don't think I will. Bye!" I replied, going to leave only to slip on sliver of soap sneaking beneath the suds. Horse over bollocks I landed with a crunch. Rolling over then getting up back onto my feet nothing seemed broken. The same could not be said for the hamster as the furry little fuck was flattened under my fine horse ass. I had always wondered what it would be like to sit on someone's face. I kind of hoped they would survive though. Just then the door knocked. The guards; I had forgotten how long I had been inside. Thinking fast I scraped the small body over to the drain with my hooves, then stamped it in.

"Oi times up!" The guard shouted, with little I could do to argue I left and promptly went to my cell. Gossip in prison spreads fast though. The word on the yard was the hamster had it out for me. No reason, he just didn't like me. You can't please everyone. You can crush them to death though and get rid of their body in a very disrespectful manner though. Like that politician allegedly did if I read the stars correctly. I'm a Sagittarius!

Not everyone was a dick though. I recall this one gentleman, - Adrian, I think his name was? - who was in for murdering rabbits, but between you and me, he took the fall for the dog he loved. Oh, and my currently celibate cellmate, a rather nice goat called Billy. Supposedly all he wanted to do was sell milk, but personally, I think that was code for cocaine. And how could I forget my only other brush with romance in the joint? I do believe I was grazing outside at the time when he approached me, and truthfully, he was hot! You could tell he worked out seriously. Anyhow, he got me back to his cell and asked if I would dress up for him.

"What do you have in mind?" I asked. He nodded his head in the direction of a cone-shaped party hat (but I could tell he was already horny, being a rhino and all) and said, "So, you want to fuck a unicorn? Sure. Let's have a magical time."

"Unicorn? Don't make me laugh. I want to screw a Pegasus. Now put these wings on!" That's when the deal fell through, as I had to explain to him that Pegasuses do not have horns. Not wanting to admit his ignorance, he kept me there until we'd watched his VHS copy of the 1997 film *Hercules* that he'd had smuggled in by his friend from the outside, Roland. That done and my point proved, I turned to the rhino to see him take his wrongness in, only to find he had fallen asleep. "Typical." Annoyed, but at the same time relieved, I elected to take a big spoon as payment and pissed off to piss.

Now, admittedly, my sentence was rather lenient for my crime. Then again, I was terrible at it. But in the end, I had learned a valuable lesson. Don't proposition police officers for sex.

On getting out, I concluded I should get my life back on track so to speak, and went straight back to trying to work. But with my poor life choices, no one would hire me. My only real experience was racing and whoring, and that's not exactly something you can put on a CV, so I popped back to where I was arrested, figuring it as good a hunting ground as any. During my time inside, however, the area had been rejuvenated with a Waitrose and a new theatre. This wasn't necessarily a problem as it meant a higher class of customer would pass my little corner and I could raise my prices accordingly - I am sort of a thoroughbred after all. What I got, however, was competition.

"Excuse me, stud - wanna milk me dry?" A dairy cow said walking up to me before winking seductively. Adorned in heels, stockings, suspenders and two bras duck-taped together with holes cut out for her engorged udders, she made for quite the sight.

"Well, stallion?" she questioned again.

"Did you just wink at me?"

"Looks like nothing gets past you, hay?

"Listen, I'm trying to work here so unless you want a knobbing or directions, please can you move along?"

"Oh, I don't think so. This is my turf and if you think I'm gonna give it up for some mardy old nag, you have another thing coming."

Fed up at this, I decided to kick her to the kerb and hope for the best but that just pissed her off.

"Ow! I can't believe you just did that. You want this corner that badly, fine, but I'm off to get my farmer."

"Yeah, well, just you do that, then," I said, totally forgetting that some farmers had shotguns.

The cow dealt with for the time being, I tried to get my head back in the game, luckily just in time for someone to take a chance on me. From around the corner strode the most scruffy looking old nag you ever did see, but work was work, I thought to myself, so off we galloped around to the side door of the theatre and then the other horses' dressing room. And that's when I noticed his body starting to split in half. Not wanting to say anything about it, I just made small talk, hinting towards payment for my efforts. He pulled his wallet out of his surprisingly bloodless wound, so at the very least he was clean.

"Sit down," he said, but it being a small room, I just sort of crouched.

"Do you want a carrot? I have a whole bag full," he offered, getting my full attention. (Dinner and a date, how could I say no?) Then, proceeding to stroke my mane, he drew closer, putting his carrot in my mouth and shushing me (I was starting to get into it). His fingers ran through my hair - yep, fingers. Startled somewhat as I recognised the distinctively human touch, I whinnied and kicked him into the wall where he split into two parts, yet still whole in and off themselves. Half horse half man and half man half horse, like some weird experiment gone wrong. Worried I'd killed him - them? - I trotted over and licked his face, causing the creature to let out a faint "Eugh." Remembering the other whole half I nudged it/him with my hoof and thankfully it twitched. Not sure what to do, I took a sheet from the table and draped it over their unconscious forms. Then, all being cleaned up as well as horsely possible, it dawned on me I was still inside his dressing room. So, after thinking about it for what must have been about half an hour and eating all the carrots he had brought with him, I had just decided to kick the door down when it opened and a young woman came in.

"Three minutes. Come on, come on - you're on," she said and pulled me by the feather boa I had put on in boredom. Glad to be out of there, I trotted along with her, when I realised we were heading to the stage.

"Oh."

"What's wrong?"

"I have always wanted to be on the stage"

"Okay," she said with a puzzled glare, then shoved me out. (Enter stage left I, guess). It went quite well at first, as, I had no lines and just had to play dumb as they paraded me around the stage.

"Oh, Mr. Horse, whatever shall I do? Oh, Mr. Horse, I think, I think I'm in love with the princess! Oh Mr. Horse, look out. Here comes the Dame!"

It was after about five minutes of playing along that I decided I needed the toilet (all them carrots). Forgetting where I was, I proceeded to do my business on stage and that's when the shit hit the fan - well, the dame in this instance - and in turn she hit me. Breaking character, she let out a string of expletives that would make anyone blush. Taking that as a cue, I leapt off and sheepishly made my way through the now roused audience of families and pantomime enthusiasts.

After my escape, I left it a few days before venturing back that way, only returning hesitantly as my need for money grew. Unfortunately, it would appear the situation had only escalated as in my absence. Police had cordoned off the area and a news crew had set up shop, as well. Not wanting to be recognised, I thought it best to not get any closer but, still wanting to keep an eye on the proceedings, I took shelter in the pub across the street. As luck would have it, the TV was tuned to the commotion outside.

As I walked up to the bar, the barman (Andrew) caught my eye and nodded. "Now then mate, what can I do for you?"

Getting my usual I replied: "Hi, can I get a pint of Vodka and a bag of carrots please mate?"

"No problem. Got these ones fresh in this morning," he said, handing me my carrots as he finished off pouring my pint. I paid the man and found a corner to watch the news. From what I gathered about what they had gathered, an unknown horse had sneaked into the theatre and beat up two of the actors and then continued on to ruin the performance in what seemed to be a sort of 'dirty protest'. This, of course, left people wondering what I had hoped to achieve. But equally left people applauding my actions calling me 'brave and bold for taking steps for animals to be portrayed by animals on stage and screen, as for too long we had been represented by CGI abominations and humans in frankly insulting costumes'.

Taken aback by this, I decided I needed a drink

and gulped at my vodka. I had really caused quite a conversation it seemed. That's when the barman got my attention, waving me back to the bar.

"Was it you?" he asked.

"Whatever do you mean?" I replied as nonchalantly as a horse could.

"Look, it's not every day a horse walks into a bar with a long, long face like yours, and the way you are glued to that TV, I would say you have more than a vested interest in what's going on. Go on - tell me I'm wrong."

Being found out so swiftly, I decided to tell him my side of the story and then got even more candid as I went on to tell him about my money problems and how I ended up where I was now. Seemingly on my side, Andrew comforted me and suggested something I had forgotten even existed during my time inside.

"Why don't you try the Grand National? It's on next week and I'm sure it will be full of punters, and you may even be able to get into the winners' stable, if you play your cards right."

Spirits lifted by spirits and Andrew at the promise of work and a distraction from the theatre, I thanked him.

"You know what, Andrew, I would give you a free bleew-job, but I think I don't can fit behind the bar. How you get in there anyway?" Dog, I was drunk, thankfully. Andrew said it was okay, he was happily married anyhow, but I didn't see a ring on his finger, well, unless he meant his work. And so, with a skip in my gallop and horse cock on the brain, my mind was set. This time I wouldn't cum first but first, second and third might.

With one week to prepare, the pressure was on, and it had been years since I had last been to the track so, doing my due diligence, I thought it best to case the joint and maybe do a dry run. Then again sex is rarely dry. On the next race day, I went for it. Admittedly, I didn't think I would get in the main gate without a ticket, but nothing ventured, nothing gained - and that's when I bumped into Markus again! Nope, just kidding, he was arrested for kid napping. (The act of putting a policeman to sleep.) I had seen him in prison though and we'd made up. Anyhow, I didn't get past the gate but that was just one option. I proceeded round the side and grazed on grass and weeds sprouting through the tarmac.

    I gradually made my way towards one of the fire exits and gave it a swift kick. I felt the door give way only to realise I had knocked it off its hinge. Going in as quietly as possible, I headed down the hallway the door smashed into. Then, taking a left at the end of the corridor, I followed my nose till I found what appeared to be a hub of life consisting of jockeys, horses, pigs, middle-aged women, rhinos and minor celebrities, all walking around naked in perfect harmony. Times sure had changed, I pondered to myself, but I was not here for the love-in. Having already navigated the maze of corridors, I made my way back the way I came, only to find the path blocked by a jockey and a horse.

    "Who the hell are you?" the horse said to me.

    "I'm a racist and if you don't mind, I was on my way out for some fresh air." Covering myself quite well, or so I thought, I let my guard down, only for them to point out a rather glaring inconsistency in my lie.

"Don't you mean racer?" he questioned. "Don't try to bullshit me. You're trotting out of the bloody smoking stables. Never mind the fact there are no racers wearing your colours today, and don't get me started on health and safety. They would never let you run with that feather boa around your neck."

Rumbled, I was left with one option: my secret weapon.

"I don't suppose you two would like a fuck?" Cards on the table, I waited with bated breath for them to reply.

They turned to one another with sly looks then with no words between them being spoken, the horse replied.

"Okay then."

Somewhat worried at the ease of the transaction, I followed them apprehensively outside and into an outbuilding. Shutting the doors behind us, the jockey giggled excitedly before squatting in the corner of the room behind a bale of hay. His eyes just visible over the top, I could not help but feel a bit creeped out. Deciding to ignore him for now, I turned my attention back to the horse who now held a riding crop in his mouth and had somehow donned a leather face mask.

Equally unnerved and impressed, I questioned their intentions. "What's with the riding crop?"

They both shouted at me, the horse dropping the crop to do so.

"Spank me!"

"Spank him!"

"Spank me!"

"Spank him!"

Still none the wiser, I just stared at the horse until he dropped his enthusiastic chant.

"I like being spanked, and as for Sid over there, well, he just wants to watch."

"Spank him!" Sid interrupted.

The horse said, "Shut up, Sid, or no cake,' and then turned to me and remorsefully added, 'I said I would treat him for his birthday, but I'm skint at the moment." All the while, Sid muttered in the corner - hopefully still dressed. Not wanting to be a Dom, I was not entirely sure what to do. Frankly, Sid gave me the willies, which was something I would never want off him. Doing what I do fourth-best, I improvised. "You know, before, when you mentioned my feather boa?"

"Yes?"

"How do you feel about being choked?" I said.

"Choke him!" Sid shouted as he popped up from behind the hay in my peripheral vision, bollock-naked.

And then followed swiftly by the horse shouting:

"Choke me!"

And so I did, until the horse eventually surrendered to my feather boa's inconceivable power! I then gently lowered him to the floor, kissed him good night and wished him sweet dreams before making for the door - only to be stopped by the still naked Sid.

"Do me, do me!" he shouted, his voice dry and desperate.

Now to be fair, I could have done but I really should have been gone by then. So, feather boa in mouth, I just walked past him. Besides, my favourite TV show was coming on soon. On the way home, however, I couldn't help thinking about how smoothly things were going. I mean they could have been worse, right?

MULEAN

After Thomas left, I decided to follow my dreams, as small as they were, and moved out to the coast for some of that fresh sea air. Unfortunately, money being an issue, I ended up in a small caravan in Seamer, but as far as I was concerned, it was the fact it was all mine that made it my home. Knowing that it was hardly ideal for a fresh start, I thought I should probably get a job and start saving so I could afford a house that rivalled whatever luxurious pad my brother had ended up in. So, walking the front, I started with the arcades and worked my way up. After some time though, it became clear no one was hiring a donkey in Scarborough. Dejected, I bought myself a bottle of cider and sat on the beach for what seemed like days, months, years, centuries, until the sun burnt out and the earth died, but I'm probably just being overly dramatic for levity.

Waking up the next morning, I was preparing to head off back to my caravan when a man and a little boy approached me and asked me, "How much?"

Confused, I asked, "How much for what?"

Evidently, some lout had attached a sign to me while I slept that said 'donkey rides'. So, bargaining with the man for ten pounds, I took the child up and down the beach a couple of times and that's how, before I knew it, I had acquired a line of screaming sticky brats wanting to ride me. It was entirely terrible, their little paws running through my hair to the point I had sleepless nights about it, and the screaming almost permanently ruined my hearing.

So, after one child too many, I quit, cold, and sodded off home, back to the family farm, which in retrospect probably saved my life, after it was announced about that egg on the TV.

On arriving I found post piled up through the door, bills upon bills. I knew I had forgotten something so, thinking on my four feet, I made the only logical leap given my experience and began offering taxi rides. Well, I wanted to, but I could not fit in the car. I could, however, be the car and so, with a higher class of clientele than the children, I commenced my new venture.

The first week was slow and bumpy going as I had no suspension and, being a donkey, my engine had no horsepower, so to speak. That's when I began running again like I did as a child growing up with my brother. Slowly the complaints stopped, and my clients started getting to their meetings on time. It was doing this that got the attention of one particular businessman who offered me a hefty, and well above normal, fee to take him to the outskirts of an out-of-the-way village. Now, don't get me wrong. I had my suspicions but sod it, I thought, how much worse could things get?

Unfortunately, they did, as he made me an unwilling accomplice in his drug smuggling operation. The police swarmed over me with guns and a big net, telling me to come quietly. Which in all honesty was something I always did so as not to disturb Tom when we lived together. In hindsight, I think I just went into shock, as they checked my pulse to see if I was still alive when I had not moved for several hours.

Snapping out of it eventually, I explained my situation. The Police said I had cooperated fully and allowed me to make a call to Tom on the day of his big race. After wishing him all the support I could muster and telling him of my predicament, I was led back to my cell. All said and done, I was just glad the businessman didn't smuggle anything up my donkey hole.

After the court hearing, I was let out on release with a suspended sentence and I tried to get on with things. But I was fed up with all the carrying of other people's baggage when I had enough of my own, so I headed home back to the family farm.

Evidently, it was not as quiet as I had left it. Across the road having erected a grand red tent in my absence, covered with lights and frilly bits. Mesmerised by the wonder of it, I followed my green cross safety code training over to what I would later come to call a circus, and then home. It was all go with amusements and curiosities, rides and clowns, lions and fewer clowns. Brought back to the moment by a pat on my back, I found a woman dressed in a red suit and tails, the ringmaster, who I would later find out was called Samantha. She told me to go away as they were not open to the public yet. Turning from the spectacle, and even fewer clowns, I headed back out the fabric door only to be stopped yet again by a camel.

"Oi, you. You have a job?"

"No," I said with glee, as I did actually want to work.

"Great. Stuff this bra. You're my replacement. I've got to return this book or I will get a fine."

Accepting on the spot, I went with it, not fully sure what I had agreed to. Of course, when I heard the cry of children and Samantha riling them up, I realised.

"Camel rides, fifteen pounds. Have a photo taken riding, thirty pounds. The strongman does kilograms."

Faced with exactly what I'd run away from, I grew to hate that camel. Regardless, I had a job to do. Well for at least that night I did.

After the shift, I confronted the ringmaster who told me that the camel had already handed her notice in before the show, and that she was due to be fired anyhow and had no intention of returning. Making me an unwilling accomplice, yet again, as I paraded around in what turned out to be Samantha's bra. Being a donkey, however, I worked out cheaper to feed, and so she offered me the camel's job and a donkey's wage. But it was better than donkey rides at the beach, as it was only three times a day as opposed to non-stop riding and groping action. The rest of the time would be mine. So I stayed on until Samantha could find a replacement, all the while using my spare time to get faster, racing the carousel's wooden horses round and round until I got dizzy, then the last clown, the lion driving the clown car, and lastly Samantha, the ringmaster. Well, she sort of chased me as I put a wooden horse in my bed and legged it one night. I was excited, as I finally felt I was ready to step into my brother's horseshoes at the Grand National. Thinking it best I have one race under my belt, I signed up for a three-legged race at a local primary school but got disqualified, as I was not a student-athlete. So, I just showed up on the big day instead. As it turned out, there were a few hurdles I was not prepared for.

"Name?"

"Name?"

"Your name's name?"

"Oh, sorry. I was in my own head," I said, while in my head I began to swear as I had forgotten to think of a name to race under. Mr. Ed? Too old. Not a donkey? Too obvious. Red Rum! Too dead. Well, probably. But prompted again, I began to force the name out.

"Red Buuuummmmm," I said stretching out the last of it to a bemused look from the organiser.

"Red Bum. Well, you do look like a bit of an arse," he said.

Nearly kicking the man for the slur, I figured it best I move on, only for him to stop me yet again.

"Hold up. Not done yet. Jockey or no jockey?"

"No jockey."

"Great. And last question - smoking or non-smoking?"

After being shown to the smoking stables, I made myself comfortable, and took my donkey shoes off and put my trainers on. I then watched as the rest of the smoking stable filled up with horses and jockeys and what appeared to be a few more oddballs like me, including a camel.

THE GRAND NUSIANCE

Milo

Not able to tell from behind if it was the one who initiated me into the circus, or a different camel, I approached with trepidation to check, but the fire alarm went off, as well as the sprinkler system, so I made my way outside with the others instead. On getting outside I looked around for the camel, eventually spotting them through the group. Approaching from behind I saw them talking to a gentleman who may have been a jockey.

"Excuse me, Camel. Can I have a word?"

"Hang on a second, hun, yes?" the camel said turning around, revealing two hairy protuberances plastered to her chest with two brass taps installed upon them. I wonded how they got there. Not the taps. The camel obviously must have seen a plumber about them. Well, I hope so anyway - nothing worse than a cowboy!

"Hi, erm, strange question, but I don't suppose you used to work at a circus by any chance?" I asked.

"No. Whyever do you ask?"

"Sorry. I mistook you for an old acquaintance from behind, but on seeing you from the front you are quite a different beast."

"Oh. Might I ask what sort of acquaintance can you recognise from behind?"

"One you regret making."

"Well, I wouldn't know about that, happily

married. Do you like my taps?"

"Shiny."

"Yes. I polished them especially for the race."

"Anyhow, I should probably get on, I will see you at the start line."

"Oh, you're racing as well? I thought you were with the press. Good luck, I guess."

"You, too."

Tom

I woke up naked in a field. Today was the big day and honestly, I was eager to work. So, after a quick wash in a pond, I began to get my stuff together. Determined to make some money, I ran through my checklist and made sure all was packed in my feeding bag. I almost forgot my Viagra, I could have kicked myself. Today was not the day to be taking chances. Setting off at a trot, I figured I could take my time. They always faff about before the race with talk of jockeys, managers and the age-old debate of whether we should replace the fences with speed bumps or automatic doors.

On my arrival things seemed quite chaotic, as a number of the entries appeared to be outside the fire exit. Curious, I watched the congregation from over the road and that's when I saw my brother.

"Milo?" What was he doing here? And why was he with the racers? He was far too slow to race and he had never shown any interest in journalism growing up. Curiosity getting the better of me, I dashed over. Approaching the back of the pack. I slowed down so as not to draw attention. If anyone asked, I would just say I was relieving myself behind a car. Genius!

I followed them in; however, it was evident I went into the wrong stables, as Milo was nowhere to be seen, and it was pretty easy to see in the non-smoking section.

"He never smoked growing up," I mouthed to myself. This was completely unlike him. What on earth was going on? Eager to get to the bottom of this, I left for the other stables and entered, passing a cosmetically enhanced camel.

"Nice humps! And your taps are fantastic too!" I said.

"Thanks. You're the second chap to compliment me today!" she replied.

With still no sight of my brother, I made my way through the entrants and jockeys. One thing was for sure: the stiff competition here today was making me stiff, ha!

Milo

It was not the camel I was looking for and I was not sure what to do, other than loiter, having forgotten my cigarettes. I debated asking for one, but my choice was made for me as the fire alarm and sprinklers went off again. Heading outside, I decided sod it, this might take a while so approached a jockey and hinted at wanting to borrow a smoke.

"Sure is a nice day for smoking," I said.

"Do you want a cigarette?"

"Yeah, please, if you don't mind. Sorry, I forgot

mine. Oh, do you have a light as well?"

Tom

Not having any luck in the crowded stable, I eventually figured sod it, I was here illegally anyhow, and pulled the fire alarm to get Milo outside in the open. Back outside, some were not impressed with how wet they were getting. It wasn't long before I finally spotted Milo again, smoking with a police officer. I only hoped he would not make my mistake before I got to him.

Milo

The Jockey seemed rather serious and a bit confused at my questions, almost like he was humouring me. Then, from the distance, I heard a voice I had not heard in a very long time.

"Oh, my Dog - I love this song!" I said to the jockey. Turning to look where it was coming from, however, I was startled by my brother.

"Milo!" he shouted, frightening me fiercely.

"Tom, where the hell did you come from? You nearly gave me a bloody heart attack, you fool. But, my Dog, it's good to see you. It's been so long."

"I was just over there," he said, gesturing to the fire exit with his tail. "But a better question would be, why the hell are you here?"

The jockey, evidently not interested in our reunion, slowly backed away, at this point not saying another word to either of us.

"No, I think a better question would be, have you

not learned your lesson about the police? I know I did," Tom said.

"What police?" I replied, confused at the mention of the rozzers.

"Him there, your buddy who just pissed off!"

"He was a jockey."

"No, he was a copper. Wait, can you not read?"

"You can read?"

"Yeah, I learnt in prison."

"You were in prison?"

"Yeah, when I got arrested, duh! Look never mind that - how did you not at least recognise him as a police officer? You have been arrested, for goodness sake."

Tom

I got to him in time before he made a blunder and the police officer backed off thankfully, giving me room to talk without incriminating myself. It seemed Milo was involved in a sting operation and evidently never saw a man in uniform. And as for his purpose here? He was here to race, and he had every intention of winning.

"Wait, you never said why are you here, Tom. Has your leg recovered fully? Can you race again?"

I tried not to lie. Well, at first.

"No, unfortunately my leg is still quite bad. I can run a bit, but really only for a little while. I'm here with the press."

"Really? I didn't think that was your sort of thing. You never were really wordy growing up. Then, again, you did learn to read in prison. Huh, I almost forgot to ask, why were you in prison?"

Shit. Now that was a hard one, so thinking fast, I used a friend's story. "Selling milk."

"Selling milk?"

"Well, that's what I told people. Between you and me, though, I always thought it was cocaine."

"Okay. Oh, look. Everyone is going back in. Hey, tell you what, though, Tom - catch me after the race, yeah? And I'll give you an exclusive interview with the winner," he said, cutting our reunion short and going back to the stables. I tried not to scream inside: things had just gotten a lot more complicated.

"For fuck's sake," I cursed out loud when he got out of ears' reach (and he had big ears, so I left it a bit to be safe). If my brother were to race and to win, what would I do? Even if he just placed high, that would screw up my plans, but at the same time...

"Fuckity, fuckfuck, fuck!" I shouted. What the fuck should I do?

Milo

Back in the stables, the atmosphere was one of tangible anticipation. Not long now, I thought, as I began my stretches.

"Left front foot, right front foot, back feeties do the splits. Left front foot, right front foot, back feeties do the splits." Garnering giggles from my neighbours, I looked over to see what they considered stretches, and I can honestly say I did not know a horse could bend that way.

After warming up, I was raring to go and it was almost perfect timing as an official came in to give us the five-minute warning. Naturally, that's when the bloody fire system went off again.

"What the fuck is wrong with this place?" I said, and multiple voices echoed my sentiments as we walked back outside for the third time that day.

Tom

After mulling things over, I came to the one and only conclusion. Of course, I would not stop my brother from winning, and he certainly would not lose either. Battle face on, I was going to make sure that he won no matter what. But what was my plan? What did I have to work with? Emptying my feeding bag on the ground, I rummaged through my pile of marital aids and random junk that had gathered over time, and that's when I found them. Two very useful drugs.

"Oh, this might actually be fun as well!" I said aloud, almost manic as a plan began to form. I made my way around to the other fire exit to see if it had been fixed. Luck clearly on my side (then again, I do have four horseshoes), I slipped back in and navigated to the dressing rooms as before, then looked for the nearest fire alarm. Setting one off for the second time that day, I walked quickly back to the stable doors and listened for the murmurs to fade from inside then gently pushed it open. Getting to work, I proceeded to find Milo's things and make a mental note not to touch them, and then drugged the troughs and the other racers' various liquids with my special prescriptions, half for one lot, half for the other. Just in time it would seem, as I heard the familiar sound of hooves and plimsolls.

Milo

Finally back inside, no time was wasted as we were now running late, and so everyone, using their last few moments, took their chance to hydrate, some even having a quick nibble before heading out. Taking my cue from the others, I followed suit and remained doing so until we were all marched out. The track was packed. This was it. This was everything I had been training for. Made to lap the ground first, all the entries looped once slowly. I was completely in awe, taking it in as I did not want to forget the experience, as our names were read over the loudspeaker.

"Number two, Grandma. Number seven, Hassa. And number twenty-three, Red Bum!" Oh, how I wished I had picked a better name. Distracted I tripped on Grandma who'd collapsed before the gates. Strange, I thought. No time to be sleeping and here of all the places.

In my gate, I tried to get comfy while I inspected neighbours turned rivals. On my left, I was greeted by the camel. And on my right a jockey without a mount. Nodding to him, I asked.

"Excited?" To which he replied.

"Not really. But for some reason, I can't get rid of this erection." Looking down I found myself staring at the stranger's crotch, not sure whether to offer advice or simply look away. I was transfixed by his bulge. Thankfully, that was when the gates opened and he ran off, cock first.

Tom

As I watched from the sidelines after making my escape things were looking promising, as one runner had collapsed before even getting into the gates. The racers all in place, the gates sprang open and they were off! Coming up the track, things did not seem too bad at first, but the effect of the drugs soon became noticeable as another two participants began to sway and fall behind the pack, collapsing mid-step. At the first fence, it was evident the horse tranquillisers were having an impact as a jockey went to leap half-heartedly and face-planted instead. Oh well, I thought - until he was trampled by the rest and I realised I should have kept them for the bigger species. Such as the giraffe, that appeared to only get the dose of Viagra and a veiny neck. In the lead group, things were not as expected. Milo was nowhere to be seen. Puzzled, I scanned the track only to see him struggling over the fence. Worried that his biggest hurdle was a hurdle, I wondered what I could do to help when I noticed him just walk around it. He always did have the brains. After that, things picked up for him. He actually got quite fast, only slowing down for corners, collapsed racers and to give directions. Before I knew it, he was closing on the lead. As the Viagra was more effective than I first thought, with one dog walking off the track rather peculiarly, and a smorgasbord of other critters heading off hand-in-paw and quite naked. Never mind the several species of ascending size who partied off in a conga line, only for it to turn out the leaders of the pack got a dose of the tranquillisers as well causing them all to rear-end each other (no not like that). Coming up on the last few fences, the rest of the racers dropped or stopped to take care of something until four remained: a camel, a woman called Linda on a bicycle, what appeared to be a Goth clown, and my brother, Milo.

Milo

Exhausted, I was kind of surprised I had lasted so long, but I was still determined to win. But, even with the competition down to a few, I was still in last place. Pushing myself even further, I came up behind a woman on her bike and shouted to her.

"Excuse me, Miss!"

"It's Linda. Nice to meet you!"

"I'm not sure if you noticed but your back wheel..." Stopping in mid-sentence, my comments were no longer needed as the bike skidded out from under as it ran through camel shit.

"Shit!" she bellowed, sliding through the impressive pile, and just like that I was in third, coming up on a Goth clown? I was not sure I could pass him as he appeared to have massive amounts of stamina and a huge amount of excitement. But just then I heard Tom, like a voice in my ear. No, not in my ear. Over the loudspeaker.

"Milo, I don't have long. I think they sent for security. But forget that - you can do it. Run. Beat that clown ass-h..." Cut off in mid-sentence, I could only assume he had been asked to leave, when he came on again.

"And fuck Terence and..."

Okay, I thought, now I know they got him.

Looking forward with renewed vigour, my course was straight and true, I locked eyes with the clown who was looking back at me. It appeared my brother's speech had got through to him as well as me, as gradually he slowed bit by bit and I passed him. Dejected, he stopped, gradually becoming a speck behind me. All the while, the camel in front was getting bigger. Perhaps sensing a presence, or maybe she looked at the big screens showing the race from the camera car, she turned to look at me.

"Oh, hey, Donkey!" she shouted.

"It's Milo."

"Whatever. Say, you're pretty fast for a Donkey."

"Thanks, I guess," I replied. But evidently, she was still faster, the placement of her humps giving her an aerodynamic advantage. I just couldn't pass her or get even close. But that didn't mean no one could, as out of left field a cow shot up beside me. Where the hell had she been? I recalled her from the gates. Grandma! Having passed out before even starting, she was arguably just a late start as opposed to falling mid-race. Back in third, I was in awe of the speed of her as she closed the distance on the camel. My hope of winning shot, I figured slow and steady coming up on the finishing line, and resigned myself to coming in a respectable third, which I did.

I made my way to the winners' circle and waited to claim bronze. It took a while, so I looked at the screens again for any update and there was one. The cow had been disqualified, having been caught being milked before the race in the car park.

"I'm second," I laughed to myself. I did it. Well, not first, but first loser is still better than third, I could not hold back my tears at placing so high as I was paraded around one last time and back to the smoking stables. But they were empty, apart from my brother. We ran up to each other and pressed our heads together in affection.

"I did it, I did it!" I said to him.

"Yes. We did it, we did it!"

"Yeah, about that - I can't believe you broke into the loudspeaker room!"

"That? That was easy. I just used what I had left from drugging the other racers."

"Excuse me?" I said, processing what he had said. "You gave them cocaine?"

"What? No, never touch the stuff. Horse tranquilizers and Viagra."

"But why?"

"To help you," he said, a confused look crossing his face.

"But I didn't ask for your help."

"Yeah, but what are big brothers for."

"Not this."

"You seem annoyed. What's wrong?" he responded, still not getting it.

"You, you thought I would want this? Why would anyone want this?"

"I was just trying to help. I figured if you won it would make you happy."

"But I didn't win. I may not even have come

second without your interfering, but that's not the point. I ran to be like you, to prove to myself I could be as fast as my big brother, and to prove to myself I could do it alone, and you took that away from me."

"I'm sorry. I didn't know. I just wan..." I cut him off. I did not want to hear him, I was so angry.

"'I just wanted to help?' Tell that to the woman covered in camel shit! In fact, go do that now because I certainly don't want to see you," I shouted, my anger building at him just looking at me.

And so, making his way out of the stables via the open fire exit, he left, leaving me with the silver medal I didn't earn.

Tom

Distraught at my miscalculation, I wandered the streets and alleyways aimlessly, not sure how I could go on after being rejected by my brother. But it was my fault. I had acted carelessly like so many times before, and this time it had cost me the one thing I held dear. I could not go on any more. Tired of being a fuck-up and tired of life, I headed to the nearest B&Q. I bought some supplies and began my work, covering myself with white paint in haphazard stripes, then attached the lights to my legs and went to bed.

My plan had a few holes, however, as I was soon awoken by a moped crashing into me, throwing its rider nearly 20 metres away. I got up to check he was okay as I didn't want to hurt anyone else, only to discover a helmet with a robin inside, evidently fine. He scolded me viciously, though, saying he was in the middle of a police chase and to get out the road.

"Stupid bloody zebra."

Apologising to him, I thought it best I find another road and so set off to the A506, perhaps the last place anyone would expect to find a zebra crossing - or one trying to commit suicide for that matter. Then everything went black.

Awakening to bright lights, I tried to walk to them but was soon restrained. I was not, in fact, in a gleaming heaven, but looking at the light bulbs of the veterinary surgery ceiling, having woken up mid-operation. Startled I had survived and was receiving treatment, I tried to talk, only to be put back under. Things went black yet again. Out of surgery, I awoke once more and found myself on a bed, my legs strapped to the ceiling.

"Why am I still here?" I questioned aloud. Why didn't they put me down? Of course, that's when the vet came in.

"Tom, nice to see you awake. You gave us all quite a scare when you came in. Honestly, we didn't think you would pull through at first, but it looks like you made it."

"Why didn't you put me down?"

"Excuse me?"

"Why didn't you shoot me!"

"Oh, euthanasia. No need, and besides, we use an injection now. Much more horsemane?"

"Well, fine then. Do that! Give me your prick. It's about bloody time I got one."

"Ha-ha. Like I said, no need. You're all fixed.

Glued you up this morning."

"You used glue?"

"Well, surgical glue. And yes, it is unfortunately made with animals. We don't have the money for the good stuff. Between you and me, though, they were on their deathbed anyhow."

"I see. So now what? Am I to stay here forever?"

"No. Whatever gave you that idea?"

"I'm strapped to the ceiling."

"Oh, that's just because of what happened in surgery. Didn't want you wriggling round again. You can go whenever you feel up to it."

Milo

Disappointed, I explained my brother's actions to the race officials. But honestly, they didn't care, and told me, "AS LONG AS WE, THE SENTIENT, MAKE MONEY, WE DO NOT CARE IN THE SLIGHTEST ABOUT THE MORALS OF THE RACERS!"

I, however, did, and so I left the medal and wandered off to drown my sorrows in a bar in the nice part of town. I ordered a cider and sat miserably in a corner. Not for too long, though, as the barman came over and sat next to me.

"Okay there, fella?" He asked

"Not really."

"Fancy a chat about it? The name's Andrew. Nice to meet you."

And so I sat there and retold my tale to that barman. He listened to me, all the while with the strangest look of realisation on his face.

"Hang on, are you Tom's brother?"

Shocked by the mention of him by name, I learnt that my brother had been there first, in that very seat, and had recounted an equally thrilling story to the very same man not too long ago. (As well as offering him some sort of sexual favour, but Andrew glossed over that quite swiftly and, frankly, I was more jealous that my brother got to be on stage, as I always wanted to be in Hamlet but was told I did not have the chops. Sorry where was I? Oh.) All of this was new to me. That, unfortunately, was not the end of it, though, as Andrew began to look somewhat guilty and told me he was the one who suggested Tom come to the race, as he had no real source of income. This of course was quite the revelation, as Tom wasn't to know I would be there until he arrived and so changed his plans on the fly, as he truly believed he would be making me happy. Worried now about how I had left things with Tom, I made haste to find him, thanked Andrew for the information, then downed my cider and left to find my brother.

Tom

Out of the vet's, I went home to the farm, back to where I still had happy memories, and went to find some rope. Tying it into a noose with my mouth, I proceeded to set it up, flinging an end over a beam in the barn, then wrapping it around a hook. I put myself in place with the aid of some hay, then I slid my neck through the hole and kicked away my support. I began to swing, choke and whinny immediately as things gradually went dark, as my eyes watered and closed. It was then when I saw death, a dark black figure silhouetted in the barn doorway, getting closer and closer. She grabbed me by my legs to pull me down to hell. So, imagine my shock when my head began to clear and I found myself still off the ground with the noose still around my neck. Confused, I looked down and found myself supported.

"Milo?"

"Tom."

"You saved me."

"That's what brothers do."

COURT

The most prolific offender I have dealt with? Oh, I recall him well, as he went about his actions with such gusto.

"Again, I find you before me in my court for the same crimes, performed with the same enthusiasm and, again, I find myself having to escalate the example I make of you to a new high. So, on top of your ban from the city centre, you shall now be required to wear diapers at all times and will be subject to spot checks to make sure you are doing so. On top of that, you will be required to wear two sets of clothes to combat your flashing."

"Objection. Cruel and unusual punishment!"

"Denied, it is my opinion that cruel and unusual punishment is the only way to settle this at this point, as it's not just a matter of you urinating in public and flashing passers-by, it's that you take such an unprecedented amount of glee in it."

"Fine, but don't think you have seen the last of me."

"If you say so, Mr. Pee-cock."

FISHING TRIP

I like to fish
I go with my friend
Set out to sea
Every other weekend
Last week however
Things went wrong
I lost my leg
And my dear friend John
Everything seemed normal
Not a cloud in the sky
I had opened a can
To wash down my pork pie
My rod was out
Cast into the sea
John at the wheel
Was smoking some green
Then all of a sudden
My line got a bite
I began to reel in
Our tea for the night
To my dismay
It was just an old welly
Strange rubbery green
So wet and smelly
John however erupted in alarm
Chuck it back
Quick lob it far
Strange as this seemed
I went for the boot
When it bit at my foot

And swallowed me up
Now in a panic I grabbed at my knife
To gut the green menace
And save my own life
By tearing it off
John had joined me on deck
He said we should go see
If we could save my leg
And besides that
We still are not safe
Boots come in twos
He was tackled from the deck

SEX, DRUGS AND MASHED POTATO

I had been drifting for a while, staying where I could, busking with my sax to earn enough for accommodation for the night and a simple meal. That was until I met Mouse. She had been watching me from my hat one day as I played in my usual spot but, not noticing her till I finished my set, I almost shoved her in my change sock with my meagre earnings until she bit my hand.

"Ow, what the shit, you little...!" I shouted, almost throwing her at a passing bus window. But even then, in the face of my anger, she was nothing but calm and collected.

"If you're over your sulk, I have a proposition for you and a working shower," she said.

Tempted more by the shower than the proposition, I tried to calm down and hoped she was not after the cheese I kept in my other sock. (I keep it there as the smell of the sock hides it from a would-be thief. Well, usually.) So, still suspicious, I packed my stuff and followed the rodent, as she filled me in on her offer.

"I've been watching you for a while now, and I have to say you're a pretty good sax blower. I think you have what it takes to be a pretty big deal. I do also think that you need a second, and I know just the bloke, as he just so happens to be my tenant, see?" So I thought at the very least I could give it a try, but I wanted to think about it and make sure I got something out of the deal other than one shower. However, it soon became apparent that she would house me and the other guy, as well as feed us, and all she asked was for us to play music wherever and whenever she wanted.

Her place had clearly seen better days, but it had a roof and the lights seemed to be on, so I followed her in. On entering, I looked around for the other guy just in case I had been more foolish than usual and walked into some sort of trap. All was good, however, and my anxiety about the situation soon faded.

"Get a wash. You stink of cheese!" Mouse told me as she left me alone to settle in for the night. Presuming I was alone, I began to get undressed and hide my precious socks before wandering around the house until I found the bathroom. The door was closed, however. I tried the handle but it would not budge an inch, so I concluded it was stuck and rammed it with my side a number of times until it finally gave, and I fell through into the bath and onto my new housemate, B.

An hour later after the police had gone and Mouse had arrived, the guy finally calmed down enough for me to apologise and for Mouse to explain her plan for us both.

"You and my new lodger here are going to form a band. If you don't like it, leave."

Her plan was quite simple, but for her to feed us and house us she must have had some faith in us.

The next few days were awkward, surprisingly so considering we had already seen each other naked, but as the week passed, we both took to our instruments out of boredom and found that we were a perfect match musically. Things were not all rosy, however. As soon as the music started, Mouse made her presence known and told us that we had a gig in two weeks. Shocked and impressed in equal measure at her capabilities in bringing us together and getting us a gig so soon, I couldn't help but begin to feel intimidated by her, despite her diminutive stature. (Then again, she did have a leather shoelace for a whip as well.) It was evident that we were not working hard enough - or at least to her standards - and so, not wanting to waste our chance, we got to work on a jazz-punk fusion piece and a cover of *Wonderdam* by The Beavers.

The time passed in a blur after that, like a speeding car, or even a non-speeding car as cars are still quite fast. Then, before we knew it, we were sort of a big deal. Our first gig spring boarded us to local acclaim and onto the circuit of mid-sized music venues around the North East. Unfortunately, neither of us were happy though, because Mouse became more a tyrant as, with our fame, she gained power.

With our only power being our selling power, we claimed we had an artistic block in order to have a rest. Believing us, Mouse relented and allowed us a break over the winter of 1999. The truth was, though, we had been worked ragged and my bandmate was not the same as he shuffled and sulked around the house, looking dead inside. And I was not the only one to notice, as one day Mouse called around with a gift for us. Potatoes. Now, I mean, yeah, they were around when we were on tour, but we never touched them as our high was performing and an early night. My bandmate, however, was not as resilient under Mouse's regime. He used what little willpower he had left to hold out 'til Mouse had left and I had gone to bed.

The next day I came downstairs to find the potatoes demolished, mashed into the carpet and the fur around my bandmate's mouth in a dry, crispy coat. Waking him to check he was okay, I was surprised to find he was the best he had been since I met him. It was like something had crawled up his ass years ago and had been controlling him, but he was finally free, you know? Unfortunately, over the next week, he took to potatoes at his leisure and at all hours. But he started writing music again and I gladly joined him, as he was happy. Mouse, however, wanted to be back in the driver's seat now things were picking up again, insisting she was vital as she had the contacts and was able to get him all the potatoes he wanted. Reluctantly, we accepted and took to the road again but, as the potatoes fuelled B's creativity, they also took what little of my friend was left away from me. Mouse didn't care though, even supplying him with instant mash. Causing him to shelve his dignity for highs, partaking in snorting the white stuff from toilet seats and even start growing his tubers in a plant pot and then eventually the local allotment. Well, until they found out what he was doing and called the police, as he didn't have a permit. That was no hair off Mouse's back though, as evidently, she had the police in her pocket now, as well. Feeling alone, and with my only comrade lost to Mouse's medication, I took matters into my own hands and did an apprenticeship to be a pest control technician. It was during that time that I learnt that the average field mouse only has a lifespan of about two years and so she would probably be dead soon, anyhow.

WALLET

Dear Diary,

Harrold almost found out today. Thank Dog I started to take them improvisation classes or I'm pretty sure I would have been rumbled. I had just taken my clothes off when we heard him open the door downstairs. He was meant to be at work.

"Have you seen my wallet?" he shouted from the bottom of the stairs as he took the first footsteps. Thinking quickly, I persuaded my gentlemen friends into the closet and chucked the chocolate bar in afterwards. I looked over to the bedside table where he usually left his wallet while picking up my top and putting it on, and not a moment too soon as the bedroom door creaked open.

"Hey, deer, have you seen my wallet anywhere?" he asked.

"Yes. You left it on the bedside table."

"Thanks, deer. Erm, quick question - why are you half-naked?"

"Oh, I sat in some chocolate and I had to put my trousers into the wash."

"And your pants, too?"

"It seeped through."

"Oh. Okay, then - let me hand you something clean. I'm by the closet, anyhow," he said.

My mind, screaming at me to think of something to stop him, blew a fuse and all I could let out was "No... okay."

On opening the closet, he was confronted with my dirty secret.

"Deer, why is there a zebra, a cobra and a Snickers chocolate bar in the closet?"

Shaking myself for my idiocy, I responded with terrible puns.

"They're my new undergarments."

Confused, I continued, "It's rather simple, Harrold. If you ever learned to unclasp a bra without looking at it, the co-bra wraps itself around my chest while I sit on the ze-bra so its head covers my top. It says on the packet that the neck hides your crotch so technically it's knickers as well, but that's far too breezy for my liking"

"And what about the chocolate bar?"

"I threw it in there out of anger."

"Ah, okay then. Best be off. See you later, deer."

I gave it a minute before letting my friends back out.

"Right then, lads, where were we?"

"You was riding me," said the zebra.

"I was choking you," said the cobra.

"You were sat on my face," said Mr. Marathon.

DINNER

"Table for two, please."

"Yes, certainly. This way, guys. Here are some menus for you to browse and I will be back with you in a minute."

"No, that's okay. We know what we want now."

"Okay, then, guys. what would you like?"

"Can I get a spicy roast grandma?"

"And can I get half a Piri Piri grandma and a few spicy breasts for the table?"

"Ah, erm, sorry guys. I think you have the wrong idea. We just sell chicken."

"But you're called Nandos. It's in the name. KFC sells chicken, Burger King sells burgers and McDonalds sells Clown burgers?"

"I don't think they do."

"Well, why is the clown called Ronald McDonald, then?"

"Yeah, but the burgers at Burger King aren't made of royal cows or the royal family, or crowns for that matter."

"That's just them bragging."

"Look, are you going to serve us grandmas or not?"

"No. All we have is chicken."

"What about her?"

"She's a customer."

"Well, if she's eating chicken, I want to eat grandma."

"Madam, I'm going to have to ask you to leave. We cannot serve you grandmas."

"So you're telling me we can go into a takeaway and commit acts of cannibalism, but me trying to do the right thing results in me being told to leave?"

"You could eat each other?"

"Okay, first of all, this bovine beauty is my wife, and second of all, how could we eat one another? If we are eating each other there is no one to eat the other."

"Oh, piss off. I don't get paid enough for this."

"Fine then, but I'm ringing my lawyer and trading standards for false advertising."

"Whatever."

"See you in court."

After a lengthy court battle, Nandos lost and were thus required by law to sell deceased grandmas. Fortunately, with the rise of state-sanctioned human farms, stocking was not an issue and soon roast grandma swept the nation. KFC, not wanting to be left behind, even began to sell the grandmas in a bargain bin of fried legs and breasts for nine ninety-nine. Swiftly followed by a new advert featuring the Sanders themselves. Watch as Mrs. Sanders is dunked into the fryer by the Colonel as he waves to the camera. Yum, yum. I bet you can't get tasty grandma like that at home, can you?

HORSEMEAT

My Dad says I'm like no one he has ever met. I think he's just lived a sheltered life. Quite ironic coming from me, since he adopted me. Dad was actually there to greet me that fateful day, while collecting some things from my childhood home. Not much, I thought to myself, just a couple of boxes, but in reality it's quite a bit more than I can handle, given my situation. I suppose none of this would have happened, if it hadn't been raining so heavily that morning, or if we had invested in some sturdier boxes, but there's nothing that can be done about that now.

"Hey, Dad, I almost forgot. I picked you up some sausage rolls on the way over."

"Thanks, boy. Here, swap you. That's the last of it by the way. You are officially moved out. I just hope you know what you are doing. Bloody private investigator. With your skills could have easily worked for the police, and don't try to tell me you don't love dogs. You could have worked in the canine unit."

"Look, Dad, I get it. It doesn't seem like a stable income, but I already have a case booked in for before lunch, and if it really doesn't work out, I can always go whine on the door of the police station and beg to get let in. I will probably have to change my name to Bell though."

"Fair enough... you tell me if you need help, though. Anyhow, what's my boy's first big case?"

"Well, from what I gathered on the phone, someone's rummaging through bins where this guy works and, him being the manager, he is responsible for it."

"Oh yeah? Could be corporate espionage."

"I doubt it. He says he works at a bakery, so the only things they have in the bins is stuff that doesn't sell, or food that's gone off. Anyhow, enough small talk. Got to run or I'm going to be late to the office. See you in a bit, yeah?" At that I ran off, as it had started to rain and I did not have any money for the bus - of course, I didn't get far before my dad tried to get the last word in.

"You know you're a bad boy. You know that?"

A rhetorical question no doubt, I still replied, "I know, Dad."

It was about 8:45 when I arrived at my office. I was soaked to the bone and about to go in when my box broke and a whole ball of nostalgia rolled out into the room.

"My ball!"

Okay, this may need some context. See, when I was little, I was in an orphanage of sorts after my birth parents disappeared. In that orphanage I had a ball, an old football to be precise, and it was mine. Everyone there had one thing that was theirs and no one else's; a lot of the time kids would come in with nothing, sometimes even naked. For me, that ball was my world.

I dropped everything else, picked it up off the floor and placed it on the shelf above my desk. Completely forgetting how wet I was, I shook off my coat and noticed for the first time I was not alone.

"May I help you?" I barked to the man in my office as I slowly circled around him and sniffed at his bollocks. "My door was locked. How did you get in? And you reek of blood. Where have you been?"

He said he was a butcher, hence the smell of entrails. As for his entrance, he used the cat-flap, the one I kept open as it's handy for postmen. And, if I was interested, he had a case. Someone was messing with the food he created, swapping it out and leaving horsemeat. The strangest thing was, they never showed on CCTV. Now, what can I say? I needed business, and secretly I hoped I would get some sausages to take home. So I declared I would start that afternoon.

"I have one meeting before lunch, then we can resume."

He left, and my expected client came in.

"Gregg, the baker. How have you been?"

"Frankly, boy, I could be better. As I told you, someone's rooting through my bins and taking what's left there."

"So, what have they taken? Just another man's rubbish."

"It's the principle!" he shouted. "They shouldn't go through my garbage." Like that it struck me.

"Is this all over some food?" I asked. "I saw this on TV. It's nothing new. It's your fellow man. He needs sustenance too." Ashamed of his fury, I showed Gregg to the door, where I was greeted with a familiar paw.

"Toby, my old playmate, as I live and breathe!"

I said, "What a pleasant surprise. Please, do come in."

Once Gregg had left, Toby decided to be nosey. "What's with the baker? He seems rather mardy." I admitted to him that I had been rooting through his bins. "I smelt sausage rolls in there once, and have been doing ever it since."

Toby burst out laughing, then invited me to dinner, as I was obviously brassic.

About one hour later, my hunger sated, I excused myself and headed back to the office, and that was when my world turned upside down. My door was smashed in and my ball was gone.

I checked everywhere but to no avail. I could not find my ball anywhere. Reluctantly, I gave up searching the office. Besides, I had paying work to do and I was late. So off I shot, down the stairs and through the hall, a quick turn at the end and out the fire exit as it was an emergency and I'm all for dramatics. Outside, I crashed into a stranger putting a sheep manikin into the bins of Gregg the baker.

"Sorry."

"No problem, friend. You're clearly in a hurry. I don't suppose though you know of a jeweller? I'm looking for a ring to propose to my lover."

I gave him some quick directions, then left and made for the smell of fresh bacon.

Arriving out of breath, I took a short break before tapping on the glass. Noticing me there, the butcher came from behind the counter and held the door open for me. That's when I remembered that I'd never actually got his name.

"Hello. Mr. Butcher. You know, I didn't get your name? I'm so sorry I'm late and I couldn't open the door. You know what it's like for those of us with paws. I can't drive a car either, or lift weights. Sorry, I'm rambling, shall we get on the case?"

"You can call me Conner, and that's okay. Yes, let's get on with it. Would you like to see the tapes?" Conner guided me through to the back where he kept his security system, and showed me the footage of the crime. To be frank, it was all quite strange, as the meat moved around as if it had legs. It was even a bit like watching synchronized swimming at one point as the meats coordinated to be swapped out and replaced with a similar cut. But why do such a thing? It seemed such a bother. So, I asked for a sample of the meat so I could get it tested by my father, who works in a lab. This meant I could get the results sooner. Taking my leave, I headed back to my dad's for the second time that day.

On my way over, though, all I could think about was my ball. Who could have taken it and why would they want it? No one knew it was there apart from my guests this morning, so one of them? But who would have had a motive? The butcher, maybe? He was there when I arrived and must have seen my joy at the ball as it caught my eye. Or maybe the baker? I mean, he has reason to be angry with me. But he doesn't know it's me who is rummaging through his bins. That just leaves Toby, my childhood friend turned chandelier manufacturer. But what could he possibly want with my old football? Jealousy perhaps? Either way, it was one of the three, I concluded.

Arriving at my father's just before four, I went to the door and whined to be let in. Having taken my keys back last week, he had also removed the cat-flap but he soon let me in and I told him of my setback. I gave him the meat and he said:
"I will test it tomorrow." He asked if I was okay as apparently, I looked hollow.
"I'm fine," I said. "Just incredibly pissed off. I just want my ball back. It's all I've got."
After hugging it out with dad, I left on a mission to stake out the butcher's for anyone suspicious. What struck me as most strange was the lack of a criminal, never mind the bloody motive, as the bastard seemed invisible.

Deciding I needed to go undercover, I binned my collar and rolled myself in some fresh mud before hitting the streets. Now naked for what seemed like the first time in years, I picked out a spot across the street, made myself comfortable and waited for a possible suspect to approach. As the evening turned to night, the thrashing crowds of shoppers dwindled, replaced by what could only be described as local wildlife. Litters littered a drunk fox, accosted a bouncer outside a Spoons while a hen do and a stag do started dancing with each other in a form of mating ritual. Unfortunately, this proved only to hinder my investigation as it provided just the distraction necessary for me to be put to sleep (not literally) as someone came up behind me and knocked me unconscious.

I woke from my forced sleep sometime later, to find myself leashed in a warehouse, completely alone. With no idea where or when I was, I looked around for windows - but to no avail. I did manage to make out what appeared to be an exterior door at the far side of the room. The real question, though, was whether it was confidence on their part that I would not be able to escape, or confidence on mine that I could? I would not have time to ponder that thought, as the door creaked, giving me pause, and so I slowly slumped back down to how they left me and played dead. When nothing happened, I was about to stir when, all of a sudden, a shout erupted in my ear.

"Oi, scruffy git, wake up. Our boss wants a word!" Not wanting to give anything away, I clenched my teeth and tried to play coy as I risked opening an eye. Only to find myself still completely alone.

"A ghost," I whispered to myself in awe, only for that same voice to attempt to deafen me again.

"Oi, dipshit, down here." Evidently, I'd had my hopes set too high for my captor. I course-corrected to find the voice was in fact that of:

"Conner, Conner, Conner, Conner, Conner, a Chameleon. You come and go, you come and go," I said as my suspect decided to show himself. "How could I be so dumb? You're a perfect fit. You swapped the meat, you swapped the meat."

"Shut up, I'm not called Conner!" the chameleon yelled.

"Sorry, Sorry, Sorry, Sorr..." I began to respond, only to get cut off by pain as electricity jolted through my body. Losing all control, my limbs contracted in, out and flailed all about. This was not the time for dancing, and it would appear the chameleon agreed, as he slowly took his foot off what I could only assume was a controller for a shock collar that had been attached while I was unconscious. Figuring it best I cooperate for the time being, I just laid motionless when the sensation left me.

"Good. Now play nice or I will shock you again," the chameleon said, then went on to address someone else. "The van ready?"

"Yeah, he's the only one, anyhow," a new voice said, with a relaxed confidence that left me quite worried. The urge to run overcame me and my body tensed. Which was probably my undoing as the second of my captors then proceeded to pick me up, bringing the rope and some of the wall with me, as it gave under his strength. Still not able to get a proper look at him, however, I took in what little I could, and found myself nuzzled against a big slimy chest. My new antagonist thundered through the warehouse to the door and out into the night's cool air. He stopped near what I could only assume was their van. I was jostled around some more while the chameleon looked for the keys. So, with no choices left but to fight back, or risk being taken Dog knows where, I lashed out and finally got a good look at my carrier as he dropped me to the ground.

"A gorilla," I mouthed, before letting out a terrified yelp at the sight of him. Not wanting to be a scaredy cat, however, I started small, reckoning I could work my way up. And so I promptly dispatched the chameleon with a leg swipe into the side of the white transit. As for the gorilla, I thought cocking my leg at him would only serve to piss him off so, with nothing to lose, I asked him a personal question.

"Why are you so slimy?"

"Excuse me?"

"I noticed when you were holding me against your strapping chest, you are really slimy. Also, you're completely bald! How did I not notice that? I mean I had other things going on, with the whole being stolen thing, but I mean - look at you!" I said, muddling the question.

"I shave." He said as if it was the most natural thing in the world. Apparently, though, he saw my confusion at his answer and maybe some repulsion, as he went on to elaborate that he was a bodybuilder and oiled his admittedly impressive body as it made for better photos. And as for his hair, it was receding in a rather unflattering and inappropriate place. While I tried not to gag at the information, the gorilla simply chuckled with derision before starting back on the big talk.

"Huhuhuhu. Anyhow back to business," he said. "You may have knocked out Leon, but what do you really think you can do against me? I'm one of the strongest animals in the world. Seriously, look at these muscles," He flexed his impressive guns before beating his oiled chest. I hated to admit it, but he was right. My karate was no good against such a heavy hitter, especially since my karate was all theoretical. Hell, the chameleon was a shot in the dark, it being night and all. It was then my dad arrived, as my tracking chip had told him I was nearby.

"Hey, boy. I saw you were in the area and wanted to know if you wanted to come to the cinema with me!" he shouted, pulling up, head and arm out of the window flailing like a mad man.

"Dad, thank Dog! This gorilla's trying to do something to me with that unconscious chameleon. Open the sunroof. I'm coming in!" My dad, being a good boy, opened it as I stumbled over the bonnet of the car. The gorilla was not letting things go, though, and began to give chase. Thanks to my superior agility, he got to the car too late, as I had already plopped through the roof headfirst and landed in the back of the car.

"Drive, then!" I shouted as I poked my head between the two front seats. On looking to see why we were still still, I saw that the gorilla had made it to the car.

"Boy, what should I do?" my dad said, as the gorilla proceeded to rub his oily body against the glass. Not sure what to suggest at first, I almost gave up until it hit me that we were in a car.

"Doughnuts!"

"What?" my dad responded, confused.

"Do doughnuts in the car. Or hell, I don't know, start driving in circles."

And so he did - round and round and round. Now, of course I did not expect the gorilla's grip to fail, or for the g-force to throw him from the car, but that's not to say I did not think things through as I threw up in the back of my dad's car.

"Are you okay back there, boy? Do you want me to stop?" he said to me, concern showing in his eyes in the rear-view mirror.

"No, I'm okay. It just means my plan is working. Keep driving. In fact, ram him hard up against that van." Taking to the prompt with gusto, my dad obliged, finishing his circle to put the gorilla in line with the side of the van, and proceeded to thrust him into it with as much speed as his Ford Focus could offer. Thankfully, it seemed to be enough as the impact made the gorilla let go. The collision almost totalled my dad's car; this was not the end of it though as the gorilla seemed to still be slightly conscious. My dad immediately began reversing through the empty car park. It seemed we had time though, as I noticed the gorilla's legs had gone all wobbly as he attempted to give chase, causing him to fall over at least twice. Heading away from the scene, it occurred to me that I had learned little to nothing from the ordeal other than that this whole thing was possibly bigger than I thought it was.

Watching the film with my dad, I could not help but feel I was wasting my time. But it gave me a much-needed break after the preceding antics. And so I settled into the movie - *Rats of the Caribbean* - and pondered the threat of a ship so small. My dad was kind enough to take me home afterwards and it gave us some time to talk.

"So, what did you think of the film?" I asked, as I wanted his take on the scale of the ships. Surely they were not historically accurate?

Ignoring me, he dropped a bombshell.

"I rushed the test through, by the way. As much as the meat is not beef or pork, it's not horse either."

"Is there anything you can tell me about it?"

"It's all from the same species."

With that knowledge, I asked my dad to let me out early, as I had decided I needed some air and wanted to walk the rest of the way home with my thoughts. It was on doing that I noticed something I had missed earlier: the local homeless dog I knew wasn't around. Worried, as occasionally we would hang out and talk, maybe sniff each other's butts, I decided to see if there was any clue as to his whereabouts. But when there was nothing to be found apart from his meagre belongings, I gave up for the night.

The next morning, I went back to where my friend had gone missing to see if he had returned in the night, only to find all his stuff to be missing as well. Not sure whether he had just moved on, or if it was something worse, I looked around for cameras. I only found one pointing out from the bookies so I went in and asked to place a bet on the Grand National as there were 2:1 odds on Linda and her BMX. While the ticket was printing, I remembered what I'd actually come in for and requested to see the footage from the previous night to that morning. The cashier told me that would be fine, but I would have to wait for the manager. I sat down and waited. That unfortunately wasted my whole morning, as she was not in till after dinner. By then, though, it was more her problem than mine, as I had scooted shit all over the carpet. Now somewhat reluctant to help, the manager still agreed, as long as I promised to go outside next time. I saw that as nothing but a plus as I had a thing for the charity box outside and thought it a good excuse to get to know her better. Also, I quite liked that plastic look she had and that little hole in her head made her unique and mysterious. Leading me upstairs, the manager insisted I wear a collar for security reasons, as that's where they kept all the money. In all honesty, I didn't mind it that much. We all have our kinks.

"These are the tapes," she said, gesturing at VHS tapes.

"You still use tapes?" I said, as anyone who lives in the modern world and does not have regular contact with CCTV might. This was getting to be interesting as, just like the butcher, the bookie was using antiquated technology.

"If it works, it works. Now, I'm going to leave you tied up with Ronnie here, and when you're done he'll buzz me to come up and get you, okay?"

"So, what is it we're doing then?" Ronnie said, after she'd gone. I explained the situation and he promptly got the video up using the fast-forward with great precision. Watching, I saw myself arrive last night and sniff around for clues before walking off home. The right tape established, I asked to go forward from there until somebody else showed up at the scene. It was not too long before they did. Well, I say that, but it looked like they had been to A&E first as they were clearly the worse for wear. Of course, this being a VHS tape, there was no optical zoom so, needing a closer look, I found myself on Ronnie's lap, staring with great intent at the gorilla and the chameleon as they cleared up the remaining bits of evidence that my friend was ever there. But why would they want him? Unless they mistook him for me? Realising what was happening, I yelped.

"Sweeny Todd!" I exclaimed, before correcting myself as I remembered.

"Sweeny Dog! It's all the same species."

Horrified, I left and headed straight to my office to ring Conner. That did not happen, though, as on my arrival, I found my doorway was blocked by a gorilla's ass. Presumably after sending the chameleon in first to do recon, the gorilla got tired of waiting and got stuck in my cat flap. Not sure what to do or if I had been noticed, I began to reverse away as quietly as possible only to be knocked out again.

Head pounding, I came around and found myself restrained in an all too familiar office - that of Toby, my childhood friend.

I shouted out in confusion, "Toby! Toby you around, mate? I appear to be tied up and could use a paw getting untied."

No response. I was about to just start shouting for help when Toby decided to make his presence known.

"You know, I was going to let you live for old times' sake, but then the butcher hired you, didn't he? But then again, who am I to stop you from interfering in my business? Oh, that's right, the person whose business it is! So now it's up to me to kill you." Baffled and shaken in equal measure, all I could muster was a question to hopefully delay him and get answers.

"Why, though?"

"Because I hate dogs, you idiot."

"But I thought we were friends?"

"Friends with you? Don't make me meow. I hate you more than anything and anyone else on this planet!"

"But why? I've not done anything."

"Not done anything!" Toby shouted, his spittle hitting me in the face. "You ruined a national treasure, an antique, with your playing and your slobbering and your biting.

"What the hell are you on about, Toby?"

"Oh, you stupid mutt. Of course, you never considered where the ball came from, just that they let you play with it and sure, why not? It was just a ball. Except it's not."

"Not a ball?"

"Not just a ball. It's a football and a famous one, at that."

"Well, I don't recognise it apart from my home movies. Oh - is it related to Bobby?"

"Oh, shut up or we will be here all day! The ball was not an actor, cretin. It was an athlete, a professional football on England's greatest day!"

"Stephen Fry's birthday?"

"What? No, you wazzock. The 1966 World Cup where England had its one and only victory against West Germany."

"Oh. Okay, and?"

"You ruined it! A piece of history, you carelessly treated it with affection and played with it every day!"

"But balls are meant to be played with, Toby."

"Well as far as I'm concerned, it's mine now and

as long as I live and breathe, no dog will play with my balls ever again!"

"I thought you were castrated, though?"

"The preferred term is cat-strated and yes, but I kept them. They were ideal for my maracas."

"The same ones you made me use in the school talent show?"

"Yes."

"You're sick."

"Well, if you took my keyboard lessons you could have used that instead, or maybe I could have just got you a dog whistle." Somewhat off topic from where we started, and still nowhere closer to escaping, I said, "I would like to leave, as I'm getting hungry and Gregg throws out what he does not sell around now."

"Oh really, well…" Toby began to say before noticing a bird had landed in his open window.

"Excuse me," it said. "Do you know which way it is to the local baker?" Toby lunged at the bird in fury at being interrupted, only for the bird to dodge and Toby to fall to the ground below. Landing again, the bird asked me, "What on earth was that about?"

Unable to think of a concise explanation I just lied. "The only way he can go to sleep is if he's cat-atonic."

The bird simply nodded and asked, "You want help getting out of that kinky setup?"

I waited as the bird nipped through my bindings, and then asked him to wait a second while I went and checked on my former friend. Rounding the corner however, all that greeted me was a small broken corpse where Toby had landed. Nothing to say to him or in his memory, I turned and headed back to the bird. We then both walked in silence to the bakers.

At the baker's, all we found was a commotion as police cars filled the street and goats rammed passers-by to move along. Curious about the presence of what seemed like half a farm's worth of animals, I went up to a police dog and asked.

"Excuse me, would you mind telling me what's going on? Did they find someone going through Gregg's bins?"

Eyeing me, the officer circled around to my ass and sniffed me for clues before answering.

"No, not exactly. More like sleeping there. Move along please." And so I did. I moved along all the way home, only to remember the problem I had left at my office.

"I'll sort it in the morning," I groaned to myself. It had been a long couple of days. There was still one thing left to do though, so I rang the police station and informed them of the events as I understood them, including the butcher's meat and my dog-napping to a warehouse at Clifton Moor, the disappearance of my homeless friend, Pat the Dog, and the accidental death of Toby. I did not realise at this point that Toby still had lives left and, in fact, had survived the fall by landing on a stray husband using the alley to piss. Then on my arrival he'd played dead, just like I'd taught him it in our youth as a way of getting out of going to school.

Oh, and I never got my bloody ball back either!

THE KING OF THE HUMBLED

Growing up, I always knew I was a little different, having two mothers and all. But there were things about me that were strange as well. I recall the day I lost one of my mothers, specifically, as it was traumatic for more than that reason. I was playing at the park, minding my business, when a gang of chicks came up to me and started picking a fight. Well, I assumed that was what they were trying to do, but they were just stating facts, saying things like 'Your mum's a cow' and 'I can hear her walking down the street'. To which I replied, "No shit. She has the little bell, you idiot," only for them to change tactics by picking on my other mother instead.

"Your mum's a chicken."

That made even less sense as an insult, despite its double meaning, as so was theirs. Which I told them. They did not see the logic through the red mist before their eyes though; they got angry and slapped me with their wings, calling me a 'big scaredy-cat' and a 'kitty with no claws'. At which point I snapped for the first time in my life. I let out a tremendous roar as I swiped at the others with my paws. This, unfortunately, gained the attention of the mother hen and she came over to begin a motherly criticism of me and my parents, who weren't even there. My emotions high, I bit her head off for biting at mine and spat it into the poultry crowd of chicks and single parents. All was not over though, as she began to run around like a headless chicken. She even made her way up the slide, albeit the wrong way before falling down the other side into the wood chippings with a small thud. That over, as she had run out of steam, all eyes fell back on to me. So I ran home. At home all was not as it had been when I left for the park. I found one of my mothers covered in blood and feathers, for one thing, tears streaming from her big bovine eyes.

"Cut!" The Director shouted. "Finally, something interesting. Ha! Look at his little face. He's devastated. Right, now when we roll, I want camera two on the kid and then Mummy, I want you to look into the camera and say a fox sneaked in through your cat-flap and ate her. Okay? Got that? Good."

My head cleared of my trauma with a snap to take in the new situation, only to discover my mother hen had been eaten while I was out, and the film crew had come back again.

"Action," The Director shouted, as a cameraman closed in for a close-up on my face.

"A fox sneaked in through your cat-flap and ate her," my mother said, devastated by the act of cruelty. I don't think there was anything she could have done, because she was too slow and big to stop him as he darted under the table and back the way he came.

Thanking the editor for showing me the footage of the accident in 4K and 60fps from three different angles and with surround sound, I took my leave and went back to my mother. The afternoon's events finally hit me and I couldn't help but wonder, what if I had been there? Could I have done something? After all, if the morning's events were anything to go by, I could have possibly made some sort of difference. Which prompted me to ask my mother, "How come I'm not like you or Mum?"

That opened a box of worms as she went into an emotional story of her and my mother from another mother who married my mother and became my mother. At this, the camera crew left for the day as, according to The Director, my mother was going to start rambling and crying again.

"I remember when I first met your mum, we were both on the debating team at university. Personally, though, I think Nat just liked a good argument. I, however, was somewhat listless and had nothing to do so found myself joining out of boredom more than anything else. Which of course led to me meeting her. From that we found we sort of completed each other. She loved my leathery docile hide, milk and little bell, whereas I loved her cocky attitude, her downy breasts and her crunchy eggs. It turned out that you were meant to take them out the shell, but Nat never told me that as I think she didn't want to embarrass me. I remember one time I even found a little plastic bag in one! I never found out how she did that," she said as she wiped her eyes on the wall-mounted towel rack.

"Anyhow, we got closer and closer throughout university until I graduated with a BSc in Aviation Technology with Pilot Studies from the University of Leeds. I had always wanted to jump over the moon, and I figured I should see if I liked flying first. Natalie, however, got kicked out in our third year for throwing her eggs at the head of the University for dissolving the debating team due to lack of members. Which to be fair was true at that point, as we used the room for some seriously heavy petting causing the rest of the team to feel a bit awkward. Then again, your mother's weight should have averaged us out somewhat."

I nodded for her to continue.

"I suppose it wasn't until after university that things got more serious, as I started doing commercial flights and Nat went to work laying for the man but, between you and me, I don't think she was ever happy doing it. She seemed to be more argumentative them days, starting fights with fast food vendors all around Leeds and threatening restaurants with legal action over petty nomenclature. Oh, that reminds me, did I ever tell you about when we went to Little Chef? She insisted the chefs must be at least smaller than her. Which led to us getting kicked out. So then she tried to sneak into the kitchen with a tape measure while wearing a rolled-up paper towel on her head as a hat to measure them personally. Sorry, I'm rambling again. What was the question?" Being a somewhat cowardly lion, I told her to continue as I was enjoying hearing about my late mother.

"I think it was around this time Nat thought it was a good idea to sign up for a reality TV show on Channel 4, sponsored by BirdsEye.

"I remember we were introduced to a pigeon and an ostrich for it. The pigeon was a bit of a twat but the ostrich was okay. Between you and me, she said she was only in it for the green card. She met the pigeon on a Russian dating site. Anyhow, it was after that she revealed the full premise of the show to me, when she asked me which one of us was going to be inseminated. Extremely confused, I asked what she meant by this? Nat hated being basted at the best of times. She explained the premise of the show being one of 'helping' couples to have babies. The show even had a tagline: 'Trouble raising the mast? No fish in the sea? Birdseye's Artificial Insemination, insensitively advertised. BirdsEye: basting babies since 1806!'

"Naturally, with that new information, I confronted your mother, only for her to break down and say that she was infertile, and her eggs were never any good, hence her recklessness with them. But she still wanted children one day, like I did, and so when the opportunity for the show came up, she jumped at the chance without asking me. The show would pay for the normally expensive procedure and even help us find a sperm donor. And at that eggshell being dropped, how could I be mad? She just wanted to give us the family we had often talked about having."

Realizing I was only at the tip of the iceberg, I had to know more. I had never even thought about having a father in my life and how I how I had such odd characteristics compared to my mothers. More curious than when we started, I asked her to continue.

"Settling into things with the cameras took some time but, at the end of the day, it was an investment of sorts so we could have you. I remember that they made us film things out of order, saying the sooner I was pregnant the better. So after we chose me to do the deed, they took us to this sperm bank which was a lot more like a regular bank than I expected, only for it to turn out we were in the NatWest across the street. That mishap out of the way, they just sat us down in front of a computer full of profiles and told us to pick someone we liked the look of. I do believe we actually took quite a while doing this, as Nat was insistent on finding someone like your dad turned out to be, and that none of the others would do. There were all sorts: ex-racehorses, ex-politicians, ex-X Factor contestants, Martins from Middleborough and Badgers from Birmingham. It wasn't until a month later that we found your dad, a lion who ran some sort of bar chain up and down the country.

"And so the next step of production began. They took us to some sort of film barn decorated like a hospital. They were obviously not ready for us, as I remember Nat pointing out a wet paint sign on the white walls of the set. This led to us engaging in a bit of small talk with the ostrich, as the pigeon was still being a bit of a twat. It turned out that the pigeon was the one they were inseminating. The ostrich told us this with an amused look. We both found it hilarious as they had picked an elephant to do the deed. Our small talk was interrupted, however, when The Director yelled, 'Action!' So, choosing to get it over with, I went and—"

Interrupting my mother I said, "You can skip this part." Even at my young age, I was maturing quite fast, and just did not want to hear that. So she skipped the waiting game to about nine months later.

"It was about the time I was due, and me and Nat had just been at Nandos as I had a craving for grandmas. As we left I felt my waters burst and so we made our way to the vet's. Neither of us was able to drive, so we ended up flagging down a man in a van as I would not fit in the back of a taxi with the camera crew still following us. We made great time though, as the man did not give a shit about following the traffic laws. Looking at the clock in reception, we realized we had arrived before we set off! Now that's when they separated us, carrying me off with a forklift to the maternity barn while Nat signed us in. I returned a minute later having given birth to an egg with a little red lion printed on it, which, according to the film crew was really anticlimactic. Meanwhile the pigeon had popped trying to give birth to the ostrich egg. But there was nothing that could be done, and we settled into the next part of filming: the incubation. Leaving Nat to be the breadwinner, I had to keep little old you warm. Scared to sit on you, though, I was left with one option - my mouth. But given my former habit of eating Nat's eggs, I was scared of that, too. Nat insisted I was being paranoid, and reassured me that I was more mindful than I thought and would never willingly hurt a child. And so I took to keeping you in my mouth like a gobstopper, sucking on your egg and licking it with my tongue while I grazed until the day you hatched out. Regrettably still inside my mouth at the time. After you broke free of your egg, you clawed at my gums and cheeks. Of course, even that still did not please the film crew, but at that point it did not really matter, as you had been born and there was not much else they could do about it."

Just then my mum's story was interrupted by

the police arriving. They took me outside whilst they got my mother's statement and distracted me with a lollipop and ride in the police horsebox. It was during this that I thought about all my mothers had been through just to have me, and how some fox could just come and take her from us, and how I wanted blood for blood.

One week later, everything was trying to get back to some semblance of normality without my mother, despite the camera crew's nosiness. But we were changed by her death and understandably so.

"And I think more so than my other mother knew," I said to Camera Two.

She took to watching *Chicken Run* on repeat all day, and I took to training in secret. Being inspired by an Italian stallion in a boxing movie I saw once, I set up a deal with a local butcher, which went quite well at first. That is until I found the raw meat too irresistible to keep my paws off. So I quit and took up jogging instead. I even trained my poor excuse for chicken wings that I had inherited off my mother, but I still could not fly when I was done. Eventually, with no sign of the fox returning, I gave up training

. I grew up and moved away from home, and started a welding company making metal gates.

"Cut." Oh, and the film crew came with me as well.

Having finished with my mothers, they'd decided to follow me as fresh meat for the show and, reluctantly, I let them follow and film me as I worked making gates. That was until one day when we saw a fox hunt through the neighbourhood and my need for revenge took over again. Giving chase, I found I had let myself get out of shape. But fortunately for me, the camera crew had wheels and were more than willing to lend them to me if it meant they could film a chase sequence. And so, me, the cameramen, The Director, the makeup artist, the caterers, Calvin the sound guy, and his son, who was visiting the set that day, all piled into their van and we were off.

Soon catching up to the fox's previous hunters, The Director rolled down the window to give them the finger and shout as we passed their mounts, "Make sure to watch this on Channel 4!" only for a responding gunshot to take out one of his wings and a mirror. We, however, were not that much faster than them, as the camera crew weighed us down somewhat. Not the cameras, mind, it's just one of them was an African elephant and the other a great white whale, so naturally his fish tank was quite heavy with all the water and shells he kept with his large cannon. (It was quite an impressive collection actually. He picked them up whenever he found himself beached.)

Anyhow, we overtook the hunters and the fox

became more concerned as we bit at the dwindling lead he had on his moped. He took to leading us around various estates, gradually building up more of a lead again as we had to slow for the corners, and a zebra crossing, but he had to as well, his manners getting the best of him. Making eye contact with us at that moment, I could tell how scared he was of us, and probably confused, but that passed just like the seasons, and the zebra, and we were off again.

Eventually the fox cornered himself in an alley through a wrong turn and we had him. I'm not sure who was more bloodthirsty at this point, me or The Director. He brushed some lint off me and pushed me out the van saying: "Go get him, champ!"

Stumbling somewhat on exiting the van, I quickly tried to regain my composure and some sort of ability to intimidate by showing my teeth and stretching out my muscly wings. This seemed to get the desired reaction and I watched his eyes go wide in fear. A gunshot rang out and echoed in the enclosed alley and the fox slumped down in front of me. I rushed at the fox to check for life but the fox spat out blood and said nothing before dying in my paws, my revenge stolen from me by some red-coated, dishonourable predators.

"Oh, sweet. Did we get that?" The Director asked his crew before addressing the hunters. "Third act twist, baby. I love it." They ignored him and approached me.

"Better luck next time, chap. I say, though, that was quite the show. Fancy joining us? We're culling the north next week," the leader of the pack said to me.

Still angry, and still lusting for blood, I almost ripped his throat out then and there, until I thought about my late mother and her numerous legal battles, and how she would wait for the perfect time to strike.

"Why not?" I said and joined them under a white flag of peace that would, with any luck, soon turn into a red napkin of revenge.

The Director, however, had other ideas. "You want to join them? Why the hell would you do that? They took your kill. Like, what sort of ending is that? What are we meant to end on? You making new friends?"

"I have my reasons, okay? Just trust me. It's the right thing to do," I told him. But he was still sceptical so, trying to reassure him, I winked and said, "I'm going to kill them." Which seemed to comfort him.

And so, time passed yet again as I waited for another fox to show. The hunting pack were quite diverse in more than just their membership, as they liked their prey varied as well.

"Any predator can kill any prey. That's just how things are, whether it's a cat killing a zebra with a machete, or a lion killing a fox with a shotgun, we're still on top, you see?" the eagle in charge explained to me after one hunt, giving me pause to think as I had never considered using a gun. So I borrowed one from another member of the pack and bided my time until the call came in that we were hunting a fox.

Setting off, we were all in great spirits. I elected not to partake in the drinking, excusing myself by saying I would have some gin later. The Director gave me a dirty look and called me a square. On the streets, though, it was obvious I had made the correct decision as we had to stop repeatedly for him to throw up in a bin. It was during one of these stops that the fox came into view, a bedraggled specimen if I had ever seen one. Grabbing The Director by his good wing, I pulled him up onto my mount, Jenny, and set off with the rest of the hunters.

It was not long before we caught up to our target and the bloodlust of the group and myself came to the surface. I shot every last one of the hunters in the back, then took aim at the fox. Distracted by The Director throwing up again, however, I seemed to only clip him. But to The Director it was like we won the European song contest. He was that surprised.

"Atta boy, I knew you had it in you! Now go get that fox." Ignoring him, I looked over the carnage I had caused. To my dismay, I found a lion still alive, and I had run out of shells. Acting on instinct, I dismounted Jenny and told her to circle the block, while I went over to wring his neck. But The Director held me back, then ran ahead of me and whispered something in the lion's ear before shouting, "Action!" and diving behind a bin.

"Well, hello son," the lion said. "If this isn't a contrived circumstance to find ourselves in, I don't know what is."

Of course, he was not to know I knew who my father really was. I had tracked him down on my gap year. He had sold his former business, electing to start a vegetarian restaurant in Norfolk with his current wife and had some free time to meet his technical child. With his last words a lie directly to my face, I mauled his throat out and left him to decompose in peace.

All was not over, however, as the fox escaped while I was in conversation, however brief. So I waited for Jenny to return. It was in that time that I found my resolve lessen, as what I had just done sunk in and the camera crew filmed dramatic close-ups of my face and the body.

Pawing myself in the head, I came back to the reality that it was a fox that killed my mother, so when Jenny pulled up, I mounted the saddle and we set off again, looking for my revenge. We soon spotted a clue: a trail of fresh blood. Recalling my shot, I could have sworn I only just hit him, and this was far too much blood for that. Concluding it must have been worse than I first thought, I got off Jenny to follow on foot, whereas the crew opted to keep their mounts and the van/trailer/tank. It seemed that the fox had made the most of my betrayal of the hunters, as the trail led me to a small council house in the rundown part of the city. Looking around as I approached, I was not sure what to do. The Director, however, had an idea.

"Okay, here's your motivation. You have just hunted down the murderer of your mother to a house in the shitty part of town. Determined on revenge, you steal this hand grenade and this cricket bat off a handsome director, who just so happens to be filming a documentary about social housing. Then you kick the door in and have a test match."

Ignoring his suggestion, I rang the doorbell and waited awkwardly in the road. Just before I went to knock (as I figured the bell might be broken), the door creaked open and a small head popped around the door.

"Hi, can I help you?" a small fox cub said. I asked if her parents were home.

"Only Daddy, and I think he's going to be dead soon, like Mummy. What is this pertaining to, may I ask? I'm the second oldest of forty three."

Shocked at the revelation of this inner-city fox, I could not help but think about the circumstances that brought me here from my childhood home, and how there could be such great disparity between us in this country we both share. While I lived in luxury alone with my film crew, this family were crammed into this box of a house and put down by a system that rewarded the elite. Yes, my childhood trauma affected me deeply and scarred me for life, but that should not lessen their lives' value because of my bigotry for their species. They were just trying to survive, the same as I was. And what was I about to do? Enter their house and kill their parent in front of them, an act worse than the fox did to me. Quietly watching me, the cub spoke up once more.

"Excuse me, sir. Are you okay?"

Snapping my head up from my bloody paws, I looked at her properly for the first time. A cub should not have to face the enemy at the gates. And so I excused myself, making my exit back the way I came.

I noticed that the film crew had not followed me though, so I returned to The Director with a leash to get him, only for him to tell me, "I've moved on. It's not me, it's you. I mean, look at it here. It's perfect. It's so shit! They still have a Netto's, and I'm no doctor but even the lampposts look like they have depression."

And so I said my goodbyes, teary-eyed as I had grown tolerant of the film crew over the years. The Director especially, as he comforted me after my break up with my boyfriend, Enrico.

Arriving home alone later, I was not sure what to do with myself. What I thought I wanted seemed so shallow to me after so many years. So what did I want to do, then?

Help them. And so I did. I was determined to raise them past their station in life as inner-city foxes. From there I set up charities and organisations using every connection I could muster, and even if it took me going from independent Lion King, working for myself, to Burger Proletarian flipping burgers, I would make a difference.

ROOM

"What do you mean they won't let us in?"

"They said they have crabs."

"That's the fifth one. This is ridiculous. I haven't heard of this many crabs in one place since I went to university."

"I told you we should have booked in advance. Let's go to Bethlehem, you said. We can stay at an inn, you said. The crustacean convention is not in Bethlehem this year, you said."

"Well, now what, then? It's easy to point fingers."

"We could ask that donkey."

"Fine, but you do it. I'm in no state."

"Excuse me, donkey. I don't suppose you know anywhere we can stay the night? My wife is pregnant and we do not wish to travel much further tonight."

"I do, actually. I own a nice semi-detached barn that has a spare stall if you're interested?"

THE SMALL GUYS

I never used to be this bitter, this angry at the world. That came with time and the death of my friends.

"So Tony, what are you up to this weekend? Anything nice? Spending time with the kids?"

"Yeah, they're leaving the nest soon, so having a bit of quality time before they're gone for good."

"Sounds great. How about you, Dennis?"

"THUD, THUD."

"Dennis, Dennis? Oh my, Dennis! You're a pancake! Tony, call an ambulance!"

"Already on it, Benny." Peck, Peck, Peck.

"Hello, I need an ambulance. My friend was run over and he's unresponsive. I'm near the art gallery."

"Are they on their way?"

"Yeah, they're coming, Dennis. Stay with us. Tony, fly up to the roof and look out for them."

"On it. Oh, it looks like they're just down the road. They have their lights on. They're going quite fast, actually."

"Okay, I'll wave them down."

"No, Benny!"

"THUD, THUD"

"Okay, who called for an ambulance? Huh, there's no one here. Bloody prank callers. Waste of our bloody time. What the hell? Hey Sam, we parked on something. Pull back a bit. STOP! That's enough."

"What is it?"

"Nothing. Just a couple of pigeons."

From that day, I swore revenge on all motorists and

any who would use the roads so carelessly, who would take lives with such nonchalant abandon, by shitting on them from great heights.

LATE

"Honey, are you keeping an eye on the time?"

"No. Why?"

"Because you have to go and get the kids from school in five minutes."

"Oh, I didn't realise. I would forget my own beak if it wasn't naturally attached to my head."

"And don't forget the parachutes and oven mitts this time."

"I thought the children took their parachutes to school with them. And do I have to wear the oven mitts? They chafe."

"No, we forgot them this morning; we were in a rush when we left the nest."

"Fine. Do I really have to wear the oven mitts though?"

"Yes. The last time you didn't, you sliced through the neighbour boy's arms when you flew him home and caused him to land on a roof."

"Ugh, fine then. Safety first I guess."

BAD NEWS

"I'm sorry. There is nothing more we can do for you."

"So, how long do I have left?"

"Well, if you're not busy, I can put you down for lunch if that's okay? I've always wanted to try hippo."

"You know what? I think I'm going to get a second opinion."

HUNGRY FOR CHRISTMAS

It's funny how a notion comes to you at the oddest moments. For example, I was squatting in my litter box reading the newspaper the other day when it occurred to me that Santa was just a bit fish, and that got me thinking, could I eat Santa? And why did it not occur to me sooner, as it seemed like an obvious option for me. Santa had been a shark for all of my life and also he was a trespasser, so why not?

Meanwhile back at the old Claus workshop

Having not gone out to go down chimneys since last year, I was unaware how much more difficult I had made Christmas for myself. For one thing, I could not survive outside of water for a prolonged period of time, plus I had no arms and legs anymore. Thankfully, Mrs. Claus had been busy in her personal workshop. She always was the brains of the situation, and the brawn. As well as the hitwoman, but that's not important.

"Put it on."

"I don't wanna."

"Put it on."

"Why should I?"

"Because you need to do your job and you can't do that from here."

"But it hurts."

"Getting eaten by a shark hurts, but you still did that."

"Fine. It still doesn't solve how I'm going to get down the chimneys though, does it? Unless you lube me up with that goose fat we have left in the fridge."

"For goodness sake, Nick! Just take some elves with you and have them go down the chimney."

"If they are going to go down the chimney, why do I need to go with them then?"

"Because you are the one endowed with magical powers that enables the reindeer to fly, while the elves are mere toymakers."

"Uh, okay then."

Jess

The next year passed by quickly and soon the big night was upon me. Everything in place, I couldn't help feel nervous that I had not thought of all the possibilities. Waiting for Santa, I paced up and down my keyboard. Not sure when to expect him, my anticipation grew to frustration, then TV and a catnap. Thinking I had only just closed my eyes, I woke to a scream of pure terror, as a tiny body tried to crawl out of my caged fireplace. Having just woken up, I almost let him out but then I realised what it was. It was an elf.

Giddy that my cage had worked, it begged the question - where was my desired target? I went over to look at the now-dead elf in my fireplace, and noticed a pair of dangling green boots. As I watched, a tiny hand reached down to the body causing them to spin upside down and their face come into view. Making eye contact, shock swept the elves face and he let out a curse, and abandoned his apparent mission to retrieve the body of his friend.

"Shit, pull me up, pull me up," he said.

Gradually rising, he left my view until the rope he dangled on snapped and he fell into the fire, screaming like the first one had. Now wondering how many bloody elves were up there, or if Santa even existed, I got lost in thought until a shout came down the chimney.

"Oi, put your fire out! I'm trying to bring you Christmas presents, and you seem to have inadvertently killed my elves. Have you not heard of central heating?"

"Santa is that you?" I shouted back up.

"Yes. Now would you please put your fire out. I'm going to have to come down now."

"Oh, sorry. I didn't realise it was you up there. I thought I might have a Home Alone situation going on. I'll put it out now," I lied, then waited with bated breath to see what he would do. After a moment, I heard a heavy thud on my rooftop and another and another, then a grunt of effort rang down the chimney and a cloud of smoke wafted into the room. Coughing, I watched the fireplace, waiting for him to fall into view. But he never did.

"Santa, are you still there?" I shouted.

"Yep, still here. I think I'm stuck. Also, you lied. You said you put that fire out."

Not sure I could move him even if I wanted to, I decided to go to bed and sort it out the next day. Unfortunately, we both died of smoke inhalation during the night. I, however, came back to life; being a cat I still had several lives left, even after Patrick hit me with his van that time. And that's how I became Santa Paws, and now everyone in the world is my owner as I bring them presents of dead birds and occasionally a dead fish.

WHAT IS LOVE? – PART DEUX

Creating the guestlist for the wedding was fraught with danger as, naturally, through my past relationship with Sarah I had gained and lost friends of hers. I mineswept through the potential problems but then I got to her father. The dilemma was whether to avoid him and go on with my life, or treat him as family and act as if the loss was equally shared. Tim, unfortunately, could not see a problem, he confessed.

"I really do have a thing for legs." And later, he even doubled down on his leg fetish saying, "The more legs on the dance floor, the merrier." This answered a simmering question as I had wondered why he had ordered bagpipes for the ceremony, as neither of us is Scottish. Invites sent and the wedding planned, all was in place for the big day. Frankly I was nervous, even though I had experienced it all before. Tim even asked if my dad would, "Walk me up the aisle doggy style?"

I do believe that's where he would walk me on all fours from behind with a leash. I replied with a non-committal 'maybe' then left him to get on. It would seem after the leg fetish, all his kinks were coming out to play. I just hoped he didn't have a thing for gnawing on balls.

Now let's speed this up a little, shall we, as what was in the intermittent stage consisted mainly of Tim asking, "Are we there yet?" and killing yet more rabbits.

Now, most adults know it's bad luck to see the

bride before the wedding. Tim, however, said, "There is no bride to not see, so I'm already doing that by not doing that."

As for something old, new, borrowed and blue, let's just say I was not digging a hole to fill three of the requirements. I decided I'd be the bride, and went off to Whitby on a hen/stag do as despite being the bride, I had a deer as a best man, while Tim went on a tour of a sausage factory.

The next morning it was all go when I awoke from my dreams of Dracula and fish and chips. I got up, then went and dragged my best man in from the lawn outside. We proceeded to get everyone ready, which ended up being a challenge as antlers jabbed me multiple times trying to help with ties. And my mate Adam bit my toes when I nearly stood on him. Following that, we made our way to breakfast and then the church in a stretch horsebox Tim had hired for us. We arrived early and found ourselves loitering and making small talk with the priest who would just not stop talking about the cost of having a flap installed.

"I do hope everyone has been toilet trained," he said. "I would rather not have to stop the service to take the groom out to go. Also, please bear in mind where you are and do not go on the graves."

Insisting that I and all the expected guests were well trained, I found it hard not to think of Tim in his collar as I looked at the priest in his.

"Go on," I muttered to myself quietly. "Who's a good priest? Yeah, marry us. You like that, don't you? Yeah, pass the plate round for the repairs for the roof. I bet someone stole the lead, didn't they? That's a naughty boy. He's going to need a confessional."

Shaking myself, I snapped back to the priest, who was nattering on about the village fair and how he was tired of all the large vegetables being waved in his face to judge. Feigning sympathy I said, "Yeah, Tim's the same with rabbits." Which I believe only served to confuse him as he turned and headed in. About time, it would seem, as the guests had started to arrive.

It was like Noah's Ark but in black tie. About to meet and greet, I caught the eye of Sarah's father with a rather well-groomed horse in a feather boa. Nodding mournfully, I looked away as unsuspiciously as possible and cursed to myself repeatedly before scrambling to take sanctuary inside the church. After crawling through the cat-flap, I stood and dusted myself down. It seemed that Tim had invited Sarah's father after all, and he had remarried to a horse. I opted to hide in the confessional until Sarah's father passed me with his new husband. Then I ducked back outside just in time for Tim, as his car pulled up with him chasing after it. Opting for superstition rather than convenience, I decided it best he not see me so leapt into a decorative bush. Unfortunately, though, he could still smell me quite well and came over to talk.

"Alan, what are you doing?"

"Trying to be lucky."

"I don't get it."

"Go inside the church, Tim, there's a good boy."

"Okay, Alan."

With Tim now inside, I had a chance to breathe as I waited for my dad to come get me.

As smoothly as things went that morning, they still went terribly, but by the afternoon we were married and ready for food.

"Speech, speech, speech," a sheep bleated out only for the rest of the sheep to follow. I looked at Tim but he simply shrugged, apparently having nothing prepared, so I figured 'sod it' and recounted how we met.

"People always ask me how I first met Tim and I would be lying if I said it wasn't awkward at first. I remember it like it was yesterday. I was late leaving my house for work but on stepping outside I was greeted by Tim. Completely naked, his leg cocked up watering my geraniums. Our eyes met across the lawn, it was almost like a Mexican standoff but the garden gnome was there and I had long since grown out of my exhibitionist fetish.

"'Morning,' he said, that toothy grin plastering his face.

"'Yes, morning. I don't suppose you could stop pissing on my flowers, though? I'm growing them for my girlfriend,' I replied.

"To which Tim said, 'But they're my flowers. I just got them.'

"Now, of course, Tim being Tim, he didn't let it go and eventually we ended up in small claims court where the judge ruled that Tim had to work for me until the emotional damage had been healed and I grew some new geraniums."

At that point, someone's phone went off and they excused themselves. I'm not sure whose the voice was, because it was drowned out by sirens outside, and I was unable to make them out as flashing blue lights glared in my eyes through the windows. I figured it was probably nothing and continued with my story.

"Anyhow, from then on we lived together with my then girlfriend, Sarah, but gradually we got closer and closer, as Tim would get in bed with us or use the toilet while I was in the shower. But then, with the unfortunate death of my wife, we came together in a way we never had before." Not like that.

"We came first in a couples-only quiz at the local pub. And then, riding that high, we went dogging. Well, the dogging came to us really, as we were just going for a walk in the park."

And that's when our luck ran out, as a man and a horse kicked the door down and entered the room in perfect unison, with dozens of goats following them.

"Tim Collie, Alan Collie - you are under arrest for the suspected murder of lots of cute, adorable, iddy-biddy rabbits. Oh, and maybe Sarah, was it?" they said.

Shocked, I looked to Tim but he was already being arrested by the police horse, who had galloped across the room in seconds, trampling numerous guests. Resigning myself to the same fate as my husband, I put my hands out to go quietly as a goat cuffed me as well.

At the station. they took Tim's pawprints and my fingerprints as well as hair, ear wax, snot, teeth, a stool sample, semen and a cuddly toy from me. All of which I kept in separate containers in my pocket at all times.

Then they took us to separate cells. I recall mine had a nice view of the river and I thought about swimming but I hadn't brought my trunks with me. Then again, they probably would have confiscated them too. Hours seemed to pass. I got bored and took to singing to myself, then looking out the window, and then I had a good cry. What the hell had we done?

I didn't see Tim again until the day of the trial. He was in relatively high spirits though, as he dragged me by my sleeve into the bathroom for something. It transpired that he had elected to represent us both as our lawyer. He said he had a plan then plopped something into my pocket. On exiting the bathroom, he insisted that things would be okay as long as I did my part, and all I had to do was listen out for our safe word. Erm no, not safe word. I mean trigger phrase. Fetch.

"Are you okay, Alan? You look like you are about to shit on the carpet. Should I take you outside?" He said.

"No, I'm fine. Just anxious about the trial. I don't want to lose you."

"Well, you never know, I might lose you instead," Tim said, his last words before we went in. We made our way to the front of the court and sat at our little table thingy, while the prosecutor made his opening statement.

"Dearly beloved, honoured guests - and Alan and Tim, I guess. We are gathered here today to determine if one of them, or both of them, killed dozens of cute little rabbits who had jobs and families to feed, as well as Tim's ex-wife, Solomon."

"She was called Sarah!" someone shouted from the courtroom balcony, and proceeded to get howls, claps, and even some stomping from the larger animals. That only simmered down when they noticed the judge tap his phone with his finger, awkwardly balanced on his wrist.

"So, anyhow, we have evidence and a surprise guest. No, no, what was it?" the prosecutor continued, then slapped his head and said, "Testimony! Well, I think that's the right word. Sorry, I'm having one of them days. Tell you what, we have stuff, yeah?" and finished up by shooting finger guns to the judge and sitting down.

"Ha, I can smell his sweat from here," Tim said, gaining even more undeserved confidence, before taking the floor for his turn.

"Hi, everybody. I'm Tim and that's my husband, Alan. Go on, wave at everyone Alan. No? Sorry he's shy. So anyhow, we didn't kill the rabbits. In fact, I love rabbits. They taste great and as for Solomon, between you and me, she smelled like cats, so what more can I say? I don't like cats, they seem to be turning the postal service into a joke. Am I right, people?" Tim paused expectantly and someone cried out.

"You know it!"

Which in all honestly could just have been Tim throwing his voice. After that, Tim stood perfectly still and quiet, as if he had heard something. Breaking the silence, the judge prompted, "Is that it?"

Tim still wasn't moving. I called him back to the table.

"Here Tim, here boy!" This got him going again and he rushed to sit by my leg. This was going to be a long day, I thought, as the prosecutor regained some composure in his seat opposite, then took the floor again.

"Calling Tim Collie to the stand."

"Shit," Tim said, having just got comfy. He sat up and said as much, only to be told, 'Here boy,' as a guard tapped the seat of the stand with one hand and beckoned with the other. Begrudgingly Tim got up and took his time before eventually sitting on the guard's hand and letting out a, "Yes."

"When was the last time you went to a dentist, Mr. Collie?"

"Dentist? What a strange question,"

"Just answer it," the judge responded.

"Never," Tim said with a grin.

"Interesting. I don't suppose you know that we keep a record of bite marks recovered from crimes such as this," the prosecutor said, immediately gaining Tim's attention and my own. I kept one of Tim's teeth in with mine in my pocket container for good luck.

"And that the teeth marks found on the rabbits happen to match those found around your home from numerous chewed-on objects."

Relieved I had not blown things with my jar of teeth I zoned out, only to be brought back to things by Tim revealing something I didn't even know.

"Well yes, that's all well and good, but part of the

reason I have never been to the dentist is because I have false teeth. I got them cheap from a dodgy veterinarian."

Someone gasped. It was me.

"So what? They still belong to you," the prosecutor said.

"Well, see, that's the thing about false teeth - they can come out, you idiot," Tim retorted and demonstrated by spitting them out of his mouth onto the stand. Then he realised he could not pick them back up and said, "Than thumbone elf foot fem fak fin." Putting his hand on his head, the judge gestured to a guard to help.

"Thank you," Tim said before continuing on. "So, from that alone, I think it's perfectly clear anyone could have used my teeth to commit the murders."

"I guess." the prosecutor said.

"Now fetch!" Tim barked, causing confusion to pass over the prosecutor's and judge's faces. It also prompted me to action as I pulled a ball out of my pocket and threw it directly at the judge's head.

"The ball's in your court, your honour," Tim said, before picking up a microphone and dropping it again.

"Erm, Gaz? Um, I mean, prosecution, do you have anything to add?" the judge asked while blinking several times, presumably seeing stars.

"Well, maybe," the prosecutor said.

"Shabadee do do do do, erma. Oh, I know, but who would have the motive, or just the opportunity to not only kill Zara, but also the family of rabbits next door to you and the ones who lodged at Cara's father's property?"

I had always thought they had moved out of their burrow at Sarah's father's house. But if Tim had been the one to kill them, it did not look good for us.

"No further questions," the prosecutor said, and Tim was dismissed from the stand, only to grow alert at something nearby. "Calling Boy to the stand."

Confused, Tim started to go up again only to be told off as it seemed he was not the only boy in the building. The boy in question, however, seemed to be a stranger.

"Can you give your name to the court please?" the prosecutor said to the stranger.

"Boy."

"And do you recognise anybody here today, Boy?"

"Yes, that man over there," he said, his paw pointing at me accusingly.

"And where do you recall seeing him?"

"He was out the back of my office that joins onto the back of the baker's, where they keep the bins."

"I see, and what was it he was doing there, might I ask?"

"Well, I thought he was dumping a mannequin, but I was in a rush to go to work so did not pay him much attention. In fact, I only really took him in when he asked me for directions to a jewellery shop so he could buy a ring."

"Now, am I correct in stating that you went back to the baker's later as you had business with him? Causing you to go inside the then sealed-off store."

"Erm, yes, sorry about that," he said, putting his head down in shame. "I had a lot on my mind and needed to talk to him about some work he hired me for."

"Because you are an investigator, yes?"

"Yep. I recognised one of the Bill on the scene, I asked him what was going on. To which he informed me of my cock-up in letting that gentleman go. Now, to be fair, he did smell horrifically of dog piss at the time. Don't get me wrong, I'm no prude, but I do think that sort of thing should be kept in the bedroom, so I made my excuses and left."

"So, in summary, he smelt like dog piss while getting rid of the body of Laura. The body that also happens to have identical bite wounds to those on the rabbits that were your neighbours, and the ones lodging at Pauline's father's house after her death."

"They owed me bloody rent, you bastard," Sarah's father erupted from directly behind my ear.

"Ow, you dick," I muttered.

"Order, order! It's like a bloody zoo in here," the judge said. "Now, let's address the elephant in the room. No one here ordered pizza. You may want to try one of the jurors' rooms down the hall."

Thanking him, the elephant left quietly but accidently slammed the door.

Continuing on with our defence seemed pointless with the damning evidence stacked against us, but purgatory was not done with us yet as the judge had not turned his phone to silent.

"Copyrighted music playing in place of ring tone, Copyrighted music playing in place of ring tone yea yea yea, yea yea yea! Copyrighted music!"

"Why hello there. You keeping my trousers warm with that furry little body of yours?" the judge answered, in a rather upbeat and smooth tone of voice, before remembering where he was and halting proceedings. He motioned to the guards and had us taken away to separate rooms to dwell on our situation, but all I could think of was Tim. He had tried, in his own way, and even had plausible deniability with the teeth but it was obvious we were guilty - or at least one of us was. And so I admitted to everything: the rabbits, Sarah, the smell of piss and the stupid stunt with the ball. However, I demanded to see Tim before they took me away. The judge obligingly let me and Tim see each other one last time.

"Hey, Tim."

"Hey, Alan. Did we win?"

"No, Tim, I'm afraid not. They think I did it all, though," I lied, not having the heart to tell him the truth of what I did.

"But that's not fair," Tim replied, his voice beginning to whine.

"I know, mate. I know," I told him.

Only allowed half an hour, our time soon passed and we were separated again. Tim insisted that he would visit as they took me away, but he never got the chance, as after my first few months in prison I got caught up in something I had no business in, then got shanked in a vital organ and bled out in the cafeteria and died. As for Tim, I keep a watchful eye on him as a ghost. He comes to visit where they buried me, to piss on my grave and mark me as his.

As I am still his, and he is still mine.

EPILOGUE BY TIM

All dressed up I looked in the mirror
My coat seamed crumpled
But black makes me look slimmer
Never mind that though tonight is the night
I'm off to the graveyard to lay by his side
And as the sun rose I gave into sleep
Reunited with Alan and the secret we keep
We loved each other
And Sarah was a sheep

G-OATS

An average amount of time ago, somewhere off of the A64, was a small cottage where a couple of bears lived - Eddy and his husband, Rupert. They had everything they could ever want and then some. Going so far as to even make their own food, they were completely self-sufficient and off the grid, which was just as well since they were wanted for the murder of police officers nationwide. They would then make porridge with their fresh goat corpses.

HOW WE MET

"Dad, how did you meet Mum?"

"Well, I was walking to work one day when I saw her come out of an alleyway. She was so beautiful I stopped in my tracks. So beautiful, she was scary. And as she stood there before me, her hairy frame blew in the wind like a dog being blow-dried and I thought to myself, that's the sort of gorilla I want to marry. So I plucked up some courage, made myself as big as possible and put my feathers out in their most seductive fan. Then, before I knew it, we were on a date in the south of France."

MORE SURGERY

A swordfish asked me for a nose job.
It drowned.
A snake asked me for a hand job.
I slapped him.

ASHES

Working in taxidermy you get all sorts of requests, but I never thought the day would come when a family member would hire me to shove a stick up someone's bottom. I recall the day fondly, and vividly, as you would, wouldn't you? The family member in question was unassuming at first, asking me how long it would take and how robust the corpse would be after the procedure. I answered honestly but then came the big question.

"Can you stick this up his bottom?"

"Yes," I said. Then obviously I asked why, and she told me.

"Well, we were going to ask you put it through his chest at first, but his grandad died of that. And as for why do it in the first place, he was a cricket fan and an umpire for amateur games on the weekend, so we figured we would let him be part of the game he so loved in life by turning him into a cricket bat in death."

GLOBAL WARMING

"You know, if this global warming keeps up, it's going to kill all the butterflies."

"The hell are you on about?"

"Wow. How thick are you? They'll melt, stupid."

"You do realise they're not made of butter?"

"Really? If they are not made of butter, why do we spread them on toast?"

"Because we are all out of margarine... well, that and we're toads."

"Are we? Is that why we're in this Yorkshire pudding?"

"Not all holes are Yorkshire puddings, you know?"

"So, this dirty looking wet stuff isn't gravy?"

"No, it's well water, like I told you when you dragged me into this hell hole with you, trying to catch that bloody butterfly!"

REAL CRIME

It was a slow afternoon at the bank as I went about the usual, seeing to customers, opening and closing accounts, taking deposits etcetera, when a ghost in a balaclava floated up to my window and placed a note on the counter. Obviously curious, I looked down to read his pigeon-scratch handwriting and what it said:

"This is a robbery," I immediately started screaming and screaming and screaming.

"Arhhh arhhhh arhhhh ahh!" Sorry, I scared myself again. Now you must be thinking, with horns like that you should be in the police force, not scared of anything! But let me bank teller you this, I just really liked cheating at Monopoly. Anyhow, after I calmed down, I began to explain that to the ghost.

"No one would play Monopoly with me after a while and so they would not let me work in a real bank either. You know, come to think of it, it was really savvy of them to make us play that in the job interview."

Confused, he flew up in my face, clearly angry.

"If this isn't a real bank, where the hell am I?"

I hesitated but told him, "A sperm bank."

He was just like, "Oh, for crap sake."

Now, at this point, I had already rung the silent alarm and spent plenty of time messing about, so it would not be too long before the police arrived. So, of course, that's when the ghost got serious.

"What's the most expensive sperm you have?" he demanded.

"This is not a store. They don't have price tags."

Which seemed to just make him more irritated.

"Will you stop messing around? You know what I mean. Just give me your most valuable load."

Afraid, I went into the back, had a root in the freezer and found a racehorse specimen. Now, just between you and me, this particular horse is currently in jail, but I figured the ghost wasn't to know; after all, psychics aren't real. So I picked the vial up with my mouth, went back through to the front and gave the ghost what he asked for.

"Is this it?" the ghost moaned, almost disappointed, but floated down anyhow to absorb it into his ghostly balaclava. He just seemed to want something at this point and so he turned to leave. Fortunately, this was just when the police arrived. But then it occurred to me, the police were outmatched. Not sure what to do, I acted on instinct and jumped up onto my desk, shouting with all my might, "Call an exorcist. He's a ghost. Your handcuffs won't work!"

Evidently surprised by this, the balaclava turned in mid-air, dropping the sperm, and said, "How thick are you? I'm a robin, you idiot."

Processing this, I looked at the balaclava and its eyeless eyeholes properly for the first time. I was so focused on the bigger picture that I didn't take time to look around to look at the little things. As I was about to apologise for not seeing past what wasn't there, a loud bang filled the air and he popped into a bloody mess of feathers, my distraction having evidently providing the police the perfect opportunity to take him out.

A while later, after I stopped screaming, a liaison officer came over to me to go over what happens next, reassuring me that they would take care of the clean up, and even arranging trauma counselling if I wanted it. Thanking them profusely I turned to walk back in, only for Truck-kun to run me down and transport me to a fantasy world. So be ready for it! As I'm back in...

"I was a goat working in a sperm bank until one day I was robbed by what I thought was a ghost but was actually a robin in a balaclava, then, after the police took care of the criminal menace, I went to leave only to get hit by a truck and killed instantly. So now I'm reincarnated into a fantasy world as a knight and my best friend is a dragon!?!!!? NANI!!!" The OVA.

BUTTOWL VILLAGE GROSSERYS

This is the village of Buttowl, located in the middle of nowhere. It has a church, a park, a school and a shop, Buttowl Village Grosserys to serve the needs of the village. You might not notice its oddities at first but, on closer inspection, you take in the blacked-out windows and the advertisements.

"Two for four pounds on any frozen products!"

"Lottery tickets and scratch cards sold here!"

"Edible panties made fresh daily!"

And then there are the signs on the door.

"No more than two unsupervised children at a time."

"Hang trench coats over trough on entry."

The shop has been run by local long-eared owl Daniel Cliff for the last six years and he takes great pride in his work, giving the village everything it needs on a daily basis. But what does the average day look like for a shop-cum-smut emporium in the middle of nowhere? Well, we caught up with Daniel earlier this week to find out. Let's take a look.

"So, Daniel, can you tell us how you start your day?"

"Uh, yeah, can do. I pop in about 6am to get things ready. Check the stock, maybe tidy anything up I was lazy about the night before. Just generally get ready for the first customers and, if it's a day like today, I might take a load in the rear like I did this morning."

"Anal?"

"Yes, I am a bit. I like to manage it all myself. I

mean, it is just me, so I kind of need to be like anal or I wouldn't be a good manager, would I?"

"So, what do you usually get in your regular loads, then?"

"Oh, all sorts. The daily newspaper, milk, eggs, condoms, lubricant, anything that has an expiry date on it really, you know?"

At this point, the local vicar, Father Leadwick walked in and greeted Daniel in a friendly but clearly distressed manner.

"Oh, Daniel. Am I glad to see you open this fine morning, as I come to you in dire need of marital aids."

"Is that so, Father?"

"Oh, yes, my son. It would appear a local hooligan has broken into the church's shed and stolen all our donated wellies for the big wanging this afternoon at the fête. But, just when I thought all was lost, I remembered your fine selection of rubber members and inspiration struck! If we can't wang wellies, why not willies instead!"

"You do know I also sell wellies, don't you, Father?"

"Oh, of course, for the rubber fetishists. How could I forget!"

"No, mainly farmers. Have you hit your head?" Worried, I called 999 for Father Leadwick. The paramedic gave him a check over and concluded he was just drunk, so sent him back to the church to sober up for this afternoon. Emergency over, Daniel then proceeded to colour code the ball gags and organize the gimp suits by size. All was quiet for the rest of the morning, apart from the occasional purchase of bread and milk, or candles and nipple clamps. Squeezing in another word with Daniel, we asked him how he sees him his role in the eyes of the village.

"Well, I see myself and the shop as a sort of community hub here for everyone, you know."

On that note, however, we found ourselves in the company of a sad clown who made straight for the counter.

"Hi, sorry to bother you. I don't suppose you have condoms in all the colours of the rainbow? I've run out of balloons, you see, and I've got to be at the fair in half an hour." Eager to help, we stood back and let Daniel fly around the shop with gusto selecting a variety of ribbed, XXL and sterilized condoms for the customer. After also purchasing some whipped cream for cream pies, a hundred G-strings to stick up his sleeve and a ball gag for a nose, the clown left with a big smile on his face.

Talking to Father Leadwick later, I found out he had been at the wine that morning and doing shots off of Jesus's abs after finding his wellies missing. Also, he never hired a clown. So who we thought was a clown was,, in fact just another pervert in a curly red wig.

"How does that make you feel Daniel?"

"What? That I helped a customer?"

"Yes."

"Fantastic. See, it's like what my mam said to me when she quoted that advert: every little helps."

"And what about the fact he lied to us?" I asked "Hell, me, you and my cameraman stood and tied them G-strings into a rope for 20 minutes and it was all for nothing."

"Oh, I wouldn't say that." Daniel replied. "I haven't had a chance to use my knot-tying badge since I was in the scouts, and let me tell you this, it's bloody difficult when all you have to use is a beak. See, that's the thing about owls - everyone thinks we all went to Oxford or Cambridge, but most of us are just salt of the sky birds and, at the end of the day, I may have helped a pervert, but I still helped someone. So did you - and that's what's important."

FUNERAL

I had a friend round my house the other day.
Come to check after my father's funeral.
But before they left they asked to use the toilet.
Something I did not consider unusual.

All of a sudden I heard a scream.
Mr. Fisher is that you?
It seemed my father had risen from the grave.
A zombie fish from the loo.

Zombie fish
Zombie fish
We buried my father in the toilet
Zombie fish
Zombie fish
When my father bit my friend, he joined him

I had a neighbour round the other day.
Come to check I was okay after the funeral.
But before they left they asked to use the toilet.
Something I did not consider unusual.

When all of a sudden I heard a scream.
What the hell is this? Mr. Fisher,
there's a man in your toilet
and a giant undead fish!

Now lucky for him he was not bit.
But nor did I need him alive.
So I left him inside my bathroom

And waited for the fool to die

Zombie fish
Zombie fish
We buried my father in the toilet
Zombie fish
Zombie fish
When my father bit my friend he joined him

I had the TV licensing man around the other day.
Asked if my father was in.
I said he was just in the toilet
Why don't you go and visit him?

PERSONALS

Dear NorthAmericanKitty,

I am writing in response to your letter in the personals this last Sunday about a "HOT COUGAR LOOKING FOR FRESH MEAT!" - I, too, am looking for a tasty treat, as you put it. So, feel free to email me anytime at ManAdult18@gmail.com.

talk soon
Norman xxx

~*~

Dear Mr. and Mrs. Carkey,

This is in reply to your advertised gathering next Wednesday evening, as I and my partner are extremely interested in meeting up with like-minded individuals and, on seeing your advert for a "Swingers' meeting", we were over the moon with joy. So, if it's not too much trouble, please save space for me and my dear husband to join you for your night of fun.

Look forward to your reply,
Mr. and Mrs. Thimpanzee.

~*~

Dear Mr. and Mrs. Carkey,

Thank you for hosting my husband and me last Wednesday evening. We unfortunately will not be joining you again after the rather unfortunate mix-up regarding "swinging", as you like to put it, as we are in fact not bonobos, despite our similar appearance, and are not interested in "swapping for the night". We are, however, overjoyed with the lovely gift basket you sent and your rather precious card thanking us for our attendance.

Mr. and Mrs. Thimpanzee

~*~

Dear NorthAmericanKitty,

I am writing in regard to my teenage son's disappearance. Norman went missing on the 15th and he had an online conversation with you around that date concerning meeting up. I believe you may have been the last person to see him alive. Before I continue, let me assure you that I have already taken the necessary measures to report him missing to the local authorities as well as reaching out to the Lion Bar establishment you met at to review their CCTV of the day in question. In short, though, I will take your silence in this matter as unwillingness to cooperate and happily forward your details to the police.

Yours Suspiciously,
Mrs. D Price

FARM

Babies. Where do they come from? Some people say fish fairs; some say you get a government licence to raise your own free range after bringing it back from the hospital. But, in reality, most babies come from one place: a human farm.

"Hi. I'm here today with farmer and ex-MP Dominic Flensing who runs the fourth largest Human Farm in County Durham. Good morning, Dom."

"Don't call me Dom."

"Okay. So, Dom, can you walk our viewers through the process of raising a mob of humans for consumption and society? And at what point are they separated into their two branching paths?"

"Well, in all honesty, there's no difference. Just like you and me. We are both people. I just happen to be an ex-MP."

"So, what you're saying is, we are all created equal and it's just that society forces us into these predetermined roles?

"Well, unless you are turned on by coins minted between the years of 1990 to 1993, then you can do what you want."

"I see. Fascinating. So once babies are born, what next?"

"Well, we initially grass feed them up to toddler age in the fields, as that's when they start talking, and then the process gets more difficult in terms of which of the livestock goes where. We have to separate them between food and family. The families go back into the sheds, while the food is allowed exercise to keep the meat lean."

"Very interesting. Now, may I ask, why is it the ones that go on to become members of the public are kept underfoot, so to speak?"

"Well, it's quite simple really. At this point in their growth, they begin to express themselves as individuals and it's a key point in separating the weak from the competition."

"By which you mean?"

"Ones who express interest in politics."

"And what happens to the competition?"

"We ring their necks, just like a chicken. After all, our main buyers here in terms of meat are the Houses of Parliament. And they don't want any working-class scum getting a baby with humanitarian ideas and a dream of becoming a politician to make a difference."

"Now, as for the food - you let them grow into their prime. Is that correct?"

"Yes, and if you look over there you can see we have just let a group of Normans into the main field to graze."

At this prompt, we decided to go and film them in the field. They were truly majestic.

"Norman, NORMAN! Norman."

"Teresa!"

"Is that the former Prime Minister?"

"Oh, yeah. That's the old girl, all right. She comes up here to run through the fields, the naughty rascal!"

"A lot of individuals might think you keeping them naked is a bad idea as it will just lead to breeding, but you have the males castrated at an early age, don't you?"

"Yes. Ironically, it's a case where the farming was less brutal in medieval times, as royals would treat the male genitalia as a delicacy and just provide them with a chastity belt. Unfortunately, though, the British willy fell out of fashion during the war when the royals took to bigger thrills, importing the nuts and knobs of war criminals. So, with demand at an all-time low these days, we just chop them off and sell them to the pig farm as scraps."

"Waste not, want not, I suppose. Now, am I right in thinking you actually saved some for us to try as you knew we were coming today?"

"No."

Somewhat disappointed, I moved on.

"Now, as you have previously mentioned, your main buyers for human flesh are politicians, but who else chooses to partake in the flesh feasting?"

"Well, apart from a few individuals who will remain nameless, we tend to get the odd hunter type animals looking to expand their palate. And the Church of England. But they might just have started sacrificing people, you can never be too sure. Then there are our newest clients, who have asked us to start ageing our meat to the tender ages of their seventy plus."

"That would be KFC, correct?"

"Yep ,and Nandos of course! False advertising will get you like that, but it's all good for business."

After that, Dom led us over to his big, ominous shed where he kept his dairy operation and introduced us to Amber, a new employee hired through a youth organisation helping disadvantaged cows.

"So, Amber, can you tell us a bit about your work?"

"Yeah, sure. What I do is I walk along under the humans with my bucket and when I feel a drip on my head, I go up and act like I'm still stealing petrol or something."

"Fascinating. If you had to give one piece of advice to the viewers if they were doing your job, what would it be?"

"Watch out for stable boys, the dirty bastards! And don't be afraid to bite down!" Leaving Amber, we continued our tour of the facilities and even got to pet old Theresa and give her a glass of blood. Now, the viewer at home may be wondering why we are telling you all this right to your face? The answer is rather simple. We know you will not do anything to change it. Three, two, one and cut."

"You know, truth be told, I have a freshly cooked Norman in the kitchen and a rather nice wine if you want to join me."

"Oh, I shouldn't. The human meat goes straight to my thighs. Then again, I'm not a member of the Green party, so why not!"

COATS

I was watching a movie one day about a vile person who desired a coat made by dogs and all I could think was, what if the baby was on the other foot, and so I went on a trip to Scarborough, only to not win any. I however knew that it was not the source of babies and so resigned myself to stealing the children. But I would need help to pull off such an audacious crime. One call from the police later over my advert in the paper, and I concluded I should probably just hang around outside a prison and ask people willy-nilly. Eventually two robins were willing to help me, and we got to work on planning our heist.

"What I'm saying is that I cannot physically lift a human baby, as I am tiny!"

"And what I'm saying is, just try!"

"He will put his wings out, muppet!"

As it didn't go well, I sacked them and hired a white van man instead to wait as I moved the babies from the incubators to the van. Electing not to tell him his role in my heist, I simply said I was hosting a party for the prime minister and had bought the babies as hors d'oeuvres.

To which his only reaction was to shaking his head and say, "Typical. Living off the people."

Choosing a night raid, I had the man drive me there around 11pm. All the while, I thought about my new coats. When there was no sign of the guard on duty, I got out of the van and told the man to wait while I let security know I was loading up. Running off I began my hunt to find the guard and take him out of the picture. A rather simple task, it turned out, as his flashlight darted around suspiciously as he sang, "Nellie Furtardo the Elephant, packed her trunk and said goodbye to her mortgage...."

Not judging the guard, I left him to his ramblings and went to the maternity shed. Entering through the human flap, I found the light switch and did a crossword while I waited for the energy saving light bulb to warm up.

"Excellent," I whispered, when I saw how many babies there were. I had struck on a day when they had a full stock. Leaving the light on I ran back to the van to get my cart so I could carry more than one at a time, then I got to work. Unfortunately, I seemed to let the guard's singing tendency rub off on me as I began an interpretation of an old school song.

"Babies! I'm collecting babies, I'm trying hard to find the biggest and the best. Babies! Lots of lovely babies. I want a baby that is better than the rest."

But it did double my speed and so, with a song in my heart and a skip in my step, I got to work stealing babies.

On getting them home, however, the work was still not done, as I had to empty the van as well. Luckily, they were easier coming out than going in; I grabbed my snow scoop and told the man to, "Just push them out onto the lawn."

He did, after I'd reassured him he would not be held accountable for bruising. Finding it rather early at this point though, I figured it best I get some sleep before dawn and so I curled up on the wriggling bulk for a few hours. Awaking to screams directly in my ear almost immediately, it occurred to me that it had not a good idea.

"Ugh. What have I got myself into?" I moaned as I moved off the babies and into my doghouse. Who would have thought making a sweatshop would be this difficult?

Around ten years later and at work in my now well-established factory, I decided to re-watch the classic movie and it struck me I had got the wrong idea when I was a pup, as Cruella had wanted to literally make a coat from the dogs she had dognapped. Annoyed at my own stupidity I decide to start over. I stopped production and pressed the button for the factory's speaker system, to tell my one hundred and one members of staff to halt their sweaty sewing as we were shutting down the factory. This being the only life they had ever known, they asked me why and for the life of me I did not have the heart to tell them. So I burned the factory down for the insurance money with them inside.

BABE IN THE WOODS

"Hey Piggy-wiggy, here are your apples."

"Thanks, Apple Tree. Wow. Red ones this time. You sure do treat me well."

"Well, that's because I love you, of course. I can't let you starve, can I?"

"Yeah, hey, listen, I'm just going to pop over to the butcher. He has another offer for me."

"Well, you tell him from me, he's an ass!"

"Will do, love, and you keep growing them apples for me. If this snow doesn't let up, I'm not going to be able to get out for food."

At that, I ran off through the woods to my spying bush and watched as Apple Tree received a delivery of apples from Asda.

"I knew it. The lying bastard," I said to myself and so quickly ran back to confront Apple Tree.

"Oh, Pig. I didn't expect you back so soon," the tree said, obviously rattled at my prompt return.

"Hey, Apple Tree, before I forget - can I get an apple for the road?"

"Why, sure. Here. Have a golden delicious."

"I bloody knew it!"

"What?"

"You're not an apple tree, are you?"

"Whatever do you mean?"

"Every apple I have ever gotten off you has been a different one. Hell, one week you gave me a bloody pear and said sorry it was a substitute! So, tell me, what the hell are you? Do you even know it's out of season to grow apples?"

"I'm sorry, Pig."

"Is that all? No excuses, no reason?"

"I never lied to you, though. I just didn't want to disappoint you, is all."

"You never lied to me? Don't make me laugh!"

"But I am an apple tree."

"Tell that to the Asda delivery man. I will be back later for my stuff. I can't stand to look at you any more."

"But Pig, I love you and I am an apple tree. I'm just infertile!" she replied, clearly distraught.

"And you never told me. What else have you lied to me about? I bet you never climbed Kilimanjaro either."

"Oh no, I did do that on my gap year," Apple Tree said.

Confused, I asked her to elaborate, as she had no legs to speak of. At which point the truth finally came out that she wasn't even a real apple tree but a man who had been stuck in a tree costume since a school play in 1986.

Since our argument, we have decided to give things a second chance and have started couples counselling. Apple Tree now going by the name Gunter, we found that we had even more in common when he spoke the truth. We still love each other very much.

SPACE

Going to space had always been a dream of mine ever since I was young. Encouraged by my father already being in the job that excited me, I decided to apply, not expecting to get it.

Dear Levi Panzie,

I am writing to inform you of your successful application and that we have decided to overlook your family's reputation in light of your personal record of excellence. Please report to the National Animal Space Agency on the nineteenth of July 2023 for your induction to the facilities and program.

Yours sincerely,
Phillip Nice
National Animal Space Agency, Hull

Overjoyed, I packed immediately and got things ready, as well as somewhat reluctantly telling my father.

After getting settled at NASA, things went fast as I found myself pushing harder and harder in friendly, and not so friendly, competition with my peers. Shortly before our graduation from the program, a call came in about the lack of contact from the space station. With no other astronauts available, the recruits were the closest thing to ready. Summoned to a briefing on the situation, tension was high. We had been out of communication with the space station for about a week, but no one had noticed as summer left us short staffed. We were to be sent up to see if we could get a response from them with the shuttle. If not, we were to dock and enter to see what was causing the radio silence on their end. The team was to consist of three of us while the rest of the class continued their training. There was me; Charlotte, a lioness; and Mitchell, a rabbit.

"Shuttle one to station over. Come in. Shuttle one to station over. Station, if anyone is there, can you please respond? Over."

On receiving no response, we went ahead and docked with the station and, after pressurising, entered an almost pitch-black corridor. We turned our suits' lights on and found a panel which showed that systems were still working, but the lights were just not on for some reason. With air cycling the station, we took our helmets off as they were always cumbersome. But just when we were about to split up to look for the crew, Mitchell got kicked in the head by a leg of meat. The captain of the silent station's remains, severed at the thigh. Charlotte decided 'waste not, want not' and dug in but there was something bugging me. Why would the leg just be floating there? Then I remembered the gravity of the situation.

Moving on, we found the rest of him floating in a corner of the next room. Thinking it best to stick together, we looked for the light switch. They never had them by the door in these new builds. Eventually we found it and, so it could cast light on our predicament, we gathered in the control room and I made a call to Earth.

"Earth. Come in. Over."

"This is Earth. The egg's hatched. Over."

"What? Never mind, the captain is confirmed dead the rest of the station is MIA. Over."

Having done our part, we gave up on the radio. We didn't know what had killed the captain but with no one else around, we assumed it probably got the crew as well. We'd be stupid to stay put any longer, so we put our helmets on. We were ready to head back when we found it; what appeared to be a metal plastic bag with Woolworths etched into it surface. (You know, like supermarket ones that are susceptible to breaking if you overfill them or put something pointy in.) It was just floating in the passage.

"What does it mean?" Mitchell asked. Looking to each other we all shrugged.

"Never heard of it." Charlotte said.

Taking it for rubbish caught in an updraft we had caused by moving around the station, Mitchell went to grab it and, in that instant, it turned itself inside out, becoming suddenly much closer to Mitchell, close enough to envelop his entire body - and that's exactly what it did. It then compressed him down and down until he was nothing more than a screwed-up bag. Spitting the bones out, it proceeded to refill with air and floated back up to hang in the air again like nothing had happened. Charlotte, enraged at this, lunged head first at the bag, only to shoot right through, making a hole on the other side. Typical supermarket bag, I thought, as the bag dropped behind her, but at least it was stopped.

Having dealt with the imminent threat, she was turning to head back when, with greater speed than the first, a bin bag sized metal bag shot up around her from a perfectly flat, prone position. Unable to do anything, I watched on in horror as she fought it from the inside but gradually the commotion stopped as, like the first, the bag compressed what was once my peer. With no one left to wait for, I scrambled back through the station, swinging from pipes and cables, making great time with the lack of gravity. But then, on my final approach to the airlock, I heard them behind me. A scrapping cloud of bags; they had been following me through the station. Growing in numbers, all inscribed with strange and different words such as *Netto*, *Safeways* and *Hillards*. They must have been dormant on our way to the control room. But aroused now by the killing of Mitchell and Charlotte, they were looking for something else to eat.

With a final push, I swung, leapt and flew with all my might down the last stretch and through the doors of the airlock. Jabbing the close button with my foot, I stopped to catch my breath. I thought the swarm probably had no reason to guard the airlock so I was probably safe inside and while I waited for the pressure to stabilise, I laid down. All the while the bags scraped menacingly at the door. A short time later, the room beeped its microwave mimic of completion and I stood to head through. Taking a glance out the window at Earth, I thought to myself, how the hell was I going to explain this? But that, as it turned out, would not be an issue as, from behind the planet, the shape of a handle came around on either side and closed towards each other, swallowing the planet whole inside a giant bag for life for death.

Acknowledgements

I'm not sure people read these but tough luck, it's my book.

Thanks to:

Andy Milne, for helping me edit the book and giving me feedback on my stupid ideas as I worked through them, as well as running courses online during the pandemic and in person when we ventured back out.

Cath Burge, for editing the book on behalf of the Writing Tree. I have not met her in person or talked to her but from her comments she really seemed to understand what I was going for and hopefully enjoyed working on the book.

Stephen Jones, my former Occupational Therapist, for introducing me to St Nicks Nature Reserve and beginning my formal writing journey.

Emma McKenzie, for introducing me to Converge at York St John University and the writing course as well as running the Ecotherapy writing at St Nicks. The birthplace of my animal stories.

Helen Kenwright, for being a supportive tutor and encouraging my stupid ideas. Running writing classes and workshops over the pandemic as well as giving me the opportunity to teach one.

Clare Flanagan, for being one of the first people to talk to me at Converge and make me feel welcome despite being extremely anxious, and running Write On since before the pandemic and during over Zoom.

William Davidson, for his support and phone calls over lockdowns as well as running the book group at St Nicks and Converge courses over Zoom during the pandemic.

St Nicks – Nature Reserve and Environment Centre
For being a place where I reconnected with myself and other people through nature. Which inspired a lot of this book as I thought about the natural world and animals on my bus rides there and back.

Kathy Sturges, (formerly of St Nicks) for her support during the lockdowns with phone calls and giving me a safe open space to go as well as all her work with the groups I regularly attend at St Nicks.

Paul Gowland, for helping me feel comfy at York St John University around so many people as well as getting me into the library before the pandemic where I wrote some of my initial drafts.

Converge as a whole, some of whom being other writers who I don't know as well but still worked hard over the pandemic to help support me and others and for giving me a voice and making me feel like I'm respected and would be missed; well, I hope so.

About Michael Fairclough

Michael has lived in the York area most of his life. He began writing as a hobby when he was around seventeen at York College while studying art, taking the form of rhyme from his new-found interest in hip-hop and rap music through graffiti artist friends. He began writing verses about topics which in hindsight were reflective of his mental health. This continued into his time at university studying illustration, as a way to express himself.

In his spare time Michael likes to read and listen to books as well as podcasts. His interests consist of art such as sketching, painting and sculpting. In recent years Michael has begun magic again, having begun as a child buying magic tricks from a stall on York market.

Michael's writing has been described as:
"Bizarre and funny, sometimes a bit gruesome, often poignant and almost always surprising."

The same could be said about his appearance.

Other Publications

You can also find Michael's work in the *Creative Writing Heals: new writing by Converge students at York St John University*' series: 'Seven Stray Thoughts' in Volume Two, 'Commuting' in Volume Three, 'Church of the Green Cross' in Volume Four, and 'Gutterballs' in Volume Five.

Printed in Great Britain
by Amazon